this
love
hurts

WWINTERS

USA Today best-selling author, Willow Winters, brings you an all-consuming and breathtaking romance you won't soon forget.

Some love stories are a slow burn. Others are quick to ignite, scorching and branding your very soul before you've taken that first breath. You're never given a chance to run from it.

That's how I'd describe what happened to us.

Everything around me blurred and all that existed were his lips, his touch...

The chase and the heat between us became addictive.

Our nights together were a distraction, one we craved to the point of letting the world crumble around us.

We should have paid more attention; we should have known that it would come to this.

We both knew it couldn't last, but that didn't change what we desired most.

All we wanted was each other...

Do You Want Me, the prequel of this epic tale of both betrayal and all-consuming love, is included.

"The emotions Willow evokes in this are on another level. This small glimpse into the world of Marcus is thrilling, chilling, a little bit sweet and a whole lot of just wow. You won't want to miss this one."—Ky Reads Romance

dedication

I would be remiss if I didn't mention a group of women who inspire me and keep me moving forward always. I have blatantly taken quotes from these wonderful people regarding the way they talk about my heroes and placed them right in the books.

"I would gladly live in hell with him."

"I need a word that means more than love."

I love you all both for the encouragement you give me and simply for the people you are.

I hope I can give you even a piece of what you've given me.

Lots of love and kisses.

Now, buckle up! I promised you a wild ride with a tempting *tick*, *tick*, *tick* all the way up until we fall down this gripping roller coaster.

He who fights with monsters should look to it that he himself does not become a monster. And if you gaze long into an abyss, the abyss also gazes into you.

—Friedrich Nietzsche

this
love
hurts

part i

do you want me?

prologue

Delilah

H IS GAZE IS SHARP; HE HAS THE MOST piercing blue eyes I've ever seen. As I freeze where I'm standing in the middle of the aisle, the faint noise of dull music mixed with the sound of carts rolling by fades into the background. It all blurs together in aisle four of the grocery store as my grip on the loaf of bread I'm holding turns so clammy that the plastic slips.

The pitter-patter of my racing heart and my blood rushing in my ears is all I can hear.

Nothing else matters. I can feel his eyes on me. Every time I blink, I see them, surrounded by shadows.

I take my time, placing the items from my cart back on the shelves with trembling fingers. There are only four things seeing as how I just got here, a bag of rice being the first item to go back on the bottom shelf before I slowly and meticulously roll my cart to the end of the only aisle I've been down.

It's chilling, the fear that rolls down my spine knowing he's watching me. Feeling him again. *Is it fear, though?* My heart beats wildly in response to the question, fighting and railing against the decision to act calm. I can't let anyone know. I just need to get out of here... So we can be alone.

My heart isn't afraid, not like my logical side is. When the shadow is just barely seen, tall and foreboding, my stomach drops and my heart flips with recognition. It's an undeniable feeling when you miss someone you know you shouldn't. I try to focus on the sound of wheels squeaking against the linoleum floor and the noisy clang of metal from carts being lined up in order to help ground me.

"Do you need any help?" The question comes from a young man in a red vest that barely hides the nondescript black logo on his white shirt beneath it. I recognize him; I've seen him a number of times in this grocery store. I'm certain he's rung me up a handful of times since I returned here a month ago.

How did I think I could move back, even if the house is on the outskirts in the middle of nowhere, and *he* wouldn't find me? How could I be so foolish to think he wouldn't come for me?

A sinking feeling in my chest moves my hand there, and the paper list in my hand crinkles as I do. I'd forgotten all about it and as I gaze down at the blurred pen lines and wrinkled paper, I do my best to school my expression.

"Oh, no," I say and my throat is too tight as I speak. I close my eyes, forcing a simple smile to my lips and clear my throat. "I just realized something," I answer, finally looking the young man in his deep brown eyes. "I have a call in ten minutes and I'm going to take it in my car then come back," I lie, that smile staying in place although everything in my body wants me to run. Run from here, get far away from other people.

The young man, who looks like he's college age or maybe younger, offers me a friendly smile in return. "Understood," he says with a nod and returns to lining up stacks of carts with the one I've just brought back up front.

Even now, as I take each deliberate step through the glass double doors that slide open automatically as I approach and feel the cool breeze of early spring against my heated face, I try to rid myself of the memories that flash before my eyes.

The bar. The drinks. The feel of a chilled glass of white wine mixed with the scent of whiskey from the man next to me. The court cases and late nights spent getting lost in bed with a man I knew I shouldn't be with. The flirtation, rules being broken.

My heels click as I remember losing my law license, as every dreadful moment returns with the stain of blood. So much blood. Acts of passion that couldn't be taken back. The pain that's already present mingles with so much more.

Wrapping my arms around myself, I attempt to protect my body from the wind but it's useless. The weather isn't what batters me.

The remembrance of his lips on mine and the searing heat of his light touch, force a gasp from me. It's a short one full of longing, knowing those moments are now nothing more than lost ghosts of the person I was. Of the people we were before it all went to hell.

All of the memories are a cocktail that infuses into my conscious thoughts as I listen to my keys clink while I unlock the door to my sedan with a low beep that fills the practically vacant lot. From the time I entered the grocery store to now, a mere fifteen minutes at that, the sun has decided to set, casting a shade of red across the dark tree line of thick forest beyond the store parking lot and stealing the light that was here only a moment ago.

The leather seat groans and the door shuts with a loud thud. All I can do is sit here, my purse now on the console. My keys in my right hand, resting against my lap with the metal digging into my palm since I'm gripping them so tight. My breathing comes in faster and faster although I'm doing everything in my power to stay calm. *He'll be here soon.*

When I hear the click of the back door opening, the one behind my seat, I close my eyes. He didn't make me wait long.

He enters the car accompanied by a chill from the evening wind and the car rocks gently until he's seated behind me and the door is shut. His scent fills my lungs first and as it does, I remember that I've been told that smell is the sense that holds the most memory. Maybe I read it somewhere, but I've never known something to be truer than that fact is now.

When I open my eyes, his chilling gaze is on mine in the rearview mirror and my treacherous heart chokes me in an attempt to escape. It hovers at the base of my throat, pounding viciously in protest.

I did always love him. There wasn't a moment that I didn't love him.

He knows that. He has to know that I still love him; we just simply couldn't be together. We decided. We decided together.

"You said you'd let me go," I whisper, speaking over my strangled breaths.

My gaze never leaves his, even as tears prick my eyes. Not until he answers me.

"I changed my mind."

chapter
one

Delilah
Two years before

I'M NOT CRAZY, RIGHT?

My phone buzzes with my sister's text at the same time as another glass of chardonnay hits the small bar-height tabletop in front of me. The round table has a two-foot radius if that; it's meant for two people max but my purse takes up half of it. Making the point quite clear: it's my table.

"Thanks," I say and offer the waitress a smile from where I'm perched on the stool. With a small nod, the all-smiles, petite brunette in a short black dress keeps it moving. She's cute, young, and damn fast on her feet. Plus, Sandy has a good memory. Taking a sip of the char-donnay, I know she told the bartender to make sure he poured my favorite brand. Sandy's table is my go-to every Wednesday. Apps are half-priced so this place is packed on Wednesdays... but it's packed with the right people. I plant my ass in this seat in the far corner of the bar where I can see everyone else, and Sandy keeps the glasses coming.

As I told an old friend from law school once, this waitress is the only hero I need after a long day in court.

The music is easy, the lights dim, and the lemon scent from whatever they use to polish all the dark wood in here is my heaven after spending every fucking day in hell. A.k.a. Judge Malden's courtroom.

I only get a single sip of the smooth wine before my phone buzzes again, vibrating against the menu beneath it that effectively takes up the other half of the table. With most of my light coming from the simple white candle on the table, I read the text, the bright light of my phone's screen hurting my tired eyes for just a moment.

They make me feel like I'm crazy.

Swallowing the harsh truth, that our parents do that to me too sometimes, I answer my sister quickly. My dark red nails fly across the letters on my phone: *It's just the way they handle things. You aren't crazy. It happened. They just want to pretend it didn't.*

Returning to my wine, my gaze flutters from the filled glass to the front entrance as it opens. The two wooden doors with iron handles are wide, worn, and heavy.

This place isn't classy. It's a pub, more or less. But the food is good and the drinks are even better. The latter is why this place is filled in the evenings and everyone comes here after work from a block down around the corner. I've made more deals in this very seat than I can count.

Maybe I'm off the clock, but I never stop working. My job is my life.

When my phone buzzes next, I take a moment to glance around the place before looking at the text message. The white wine slips past my lips, painted the same shade of red as my nails, as my gaze moves from Patterson in his dark gray suit and then to Miller and her subordinate. Patterson's an older man who's been divorced three times now because of his workaholic and alcoholic ways combined. All three of them are lawyers. Well, the third wants to be. I don't know what the hell his name is, but she's taken the young man under her wing. Another way of thinking about it is that she's found someone tall, dark, and handsome, but dumb as rocks to do her filings.

She knows as well as all of us that he's not going to cut it. I'd never trust anyone to come within an inch of my paperwork if they can't pass the bar. A huff of disdain leaves me, but a friendly smile finds its way to my face as I lift my glass to her when her eyes reach mine.

It's short-lived and veiled mutual distaste for one another. She's as cutthroat as I am, but with two decades' more experience. Decades that also taught her she can take shortcuts and bend rules ... *bend not break*, as she once said. One day, I'll be one of the bigger names and I won't do it the way she did.

My phone buzzing in my hand is the perfect out to ignore her. Unless I'm trying a case against one of her defendants, there's no reason to engage with Miss Miller. *She's the reason lawyers have a bad rap.* I check my phone again to see a row of messages from Cadence. The summary of it isn't anything I didn't already know: she understands they pretend like it didn't happen and like our childhood was full of white picket fences and tamed rosebushes. Our parents' house may have both of those now, but that's not how we grew up.

Just ignore them, I offer her in a quickly typed message. Her response is even quicker, hitting my phone before I'm able to clutch the thin stem of my wineglass again.

The front doors open, offering some light and distraction in my periphery, but I'm caught in her message.

I love you, but I can't just ignore it like you can.

She's so emotional. My sister is the child counselor at the middle school we both went to when we were kids. Of course she's wound up over this, but this is old news. It's past pain. I take a moment to think about how best to respond, knowing she's hurting. She's sensitive and she needs more support than I ever did in this aspect of life. She doesn't get it though, and I don't know that she wants to. I text her back regardless because she's my sister, and I get it. I completely understand the struggle.

You can't change the past or the way our parents cope. I'm here for you. You aren't crazy. It happened and if you want to talk about it, talk with me, not them.

The exhaustion weighs down my expression, pulling at the corners of my lips. Hurriedly, I hide it all by throwing back the rest of my wine. Spinning the large glass with my pointer and thumb finger on the stem, I take in her messages that she's okay and that she loves me.

That's all that matters, isn't it? That we're all okay now. That's what matters. I wish she could see it like that, but she doesn't. Maybe it's because she sees them more than me. After all, I'm a state away and she only has a neighborhood separating them from her.

As I'm typing out that I love her too, Sandy takes my empty glass and replaces it with another, this one filled nearly to the brim.

"Long days deserve large glasses," she says beneath her breath with a sympathetic tone and a knowing wink. The grin I give her is wider and more genuine than I've given anyone all week. *My girl.*

My fingers toy with the stem absently as I stare at my phone, waiting to see if Cady has anything else to say. I don't know what to tell her. I don't ignore what happened or the fact that my parents pretend like everything's fine. I wouldn't even say that I've moved on. I've just simply moved forward. The past doesn't haunt me anymore. She should let it go too.

"White wine?" A deep voice from my left is followed by the sound of wooden legs grinding against the slate floor as he pulls out a stool and takes a seat. *Agent Cody Walsh.*

I wish I could have contained the jump in my shoulders and the way my heart beats wildly at the sudden sound of him sneaking up on me.

"Shit, sorry," he says and his tone is light as I laugh, letting my body sway gently as I shake my head, peeking up at him through my thick lashes. I hope my lipstick is still in place. He told me once how the dark red looks good on my light brown skin. I don't wear it just for him, but I can't deny that I like it when he sees me in this particular shade. His gaze drifts to my lips then. That's when the butterflies happen. My thirtieth birthday behind me and I still get butterflies.

Shaking it off is easy for me, but stopping this smile from growing as this handsome man eyes me ... well, that's not so easy. Neither is stopping the heat of a blush from creeping up my cheeks all the way to my temple.

"It's fine," I say as I wave him off and seek refuge in my glass of wine. Within seconds I'm in control, relaxed and myself again. I don't know if he saw the heat I felt or if he thought it was just embarrassment, but Cody is a gentleman, so he doesn't say either way.

"I just wanted—" he starts, but Sandy interrupts, dropping a double Jack and Coke in front of him. "Thanks, Sandy," he answers, his tone different. More professional maybe. My stomach doubles over in the best of ways and then that feeling travels lower as I wonder if he talks to me differently than he does to other women.

When I'm consulting with his team, it's men only. I rarely see him out of the office. Especially since they go out of town so much.

There's an obvious masculinity to the strong man in front of me. A hard edge that doesn't seem to matter whenever he flashes me a charming smile. I've spent a number of nights with a toy between my legs, thinking about him. Watching him in interrogation rooms, observing the way he works and the manner in which others look up to him, does something to me. He's only in his late thirties, maybe in his early forties, but the way he does just about everything has an air of authority that's undeniable. Being a member of the FBI will do that to you I suppose.

It's sexy as hell. As he reaches for the glass, palming it

with his large hand and takes a swig, I glance at the muscles in his forearms, out to play tonight since he's rolled up his button-down's sleeves. They sure as hell don't hurt his sex god image I've conjured up in my head.

I've been in this town in Pennsylvania since I left New York five years ago. Walsh happened to come here too from Virginia. The same case brought us here and we both stayed. Maybe it's camaraderie from the now cold case or maybe it's the mutual misery we've endured in this gray town riddled with corruption, but every time I see this man, I want to be under him more and more by the end of the night.

"Just wanted to say," he starts again, setting down his glass, the swirling amber liquid more Jack than Coke and he keeps his blue eyes focused on it rather than me for the half second. Reaching my gaze, he tells me, "I'm sorry you went through that hell yesterday."

Confusion hits me first. Then a blip of reality. Right. Of course he's thinking about business and not fucking me into his mattress.

"It was nothing."

"It wasn't nothing. There was no reason for her to bring up that shit." His tone is deathly low although there's nothing but compassion there.

"Her" meaning the reporter, a blonde with perfect hair who goes by Jill and works for the local eleven o'clock news. And "that shit" meaning the case that brought us both here five years ago.

We were both in deep, both devastated when every lead gave us nothing and the one man we could track down ended up dead. There was nothing left that we could

13

do. The murders stopped and the evidence didn't lead to anyone still living.

"It's fine, Walsh," I say, shutting down his anger with a flat tone of my own and reach for my wine again, but I don't drink it. "She's not a lawyer or a detective. She has no idea what she's talking about."

"No," he answers and waits for my gaze to meet his. My chest hollows but somehow feels full just the same when I see his steely blue eyes. "It's not fine." His last statement is almost a murmur. He's the one who breaks our stare to look down into his full glass and then empty in a second when he throws it all back.

I don't look back at him, even though I can feel somebody's eyes on me. Someone else is watching me. There's a prick that travels up the base of my neck, making the small hairs there stand on edge. I can feel it. But not a soul is looking at me when I glance around the room. A shiver rolls down my spine.

The chilling sensation doesn't stop and I have to turn around toward the small window near our table to check there too, but no one's there either.

"I'm sorry, maybe I shouldn't have brought it up." Cody's somber tone forces me to look back at him and I do what I haven't done even once in the years I've known him; I lay my hand on his. The touch is hot, smoldering even, sending a tingle up my arm that jolts me. It's only a fraction of a second before I realize what I've done and I quickly move to pat his hand, but from the look in his eyes I know that he knows a friendly pat wasn't my intention.

"It's really," I say then clear my throat and clasp my hands together in my lap before continuing. "It's fine, I promise you. I can take her criticism when I know I did everything I could."

The first thing I learned in this field is the truest statement: *everyone wants someone to blame.* If Cody doesn't catch the bad guy or if I don't get him convicted … well, then it's one of the two of us who gets blamed.

Cody's gaze drifts to my lips for just a moment; I know it's brought on because I snag my bottom lip between my teeth and maybe he notices the lipstick.

He clears his throat like I did and sits up straighter, the empty glass in his hand staying where it is since the place is busier now and Sandy is nowhere to be seen. With his broad shoulders squared, he looks straight ahead rather than at me when he speaks. "It's not your fault we didn't catch the bastard," he murmurs and for a moment I question if he meant those words for me or himself.

"You want another?" I offer him, not liking this conversation and wanting the easy air between us again.

Tapping the base of the glass on the bar, Cody pauses and then glances up at me, a boyish smirk crossing his face. "Only if you have it with me."

Just like that, all the tension is gone and the smile I had for him when he first sat down comes back.

I tell myself that I'm not like my mother. I don't forget. I don't pretend. I'm aware of my reality.

I'm simply making the best with what I've got.

Right now, that's a tall glass of chardonnay and a handsome man to keep me company. Even if I go home alone to an empty apartment and a too-hard mattress that makes the tight muscles in my back even tighter, I'm doing all right for what I've been through.

chapter
two

Delilah

SOME DAYS YOU'RE THE DOG. SOME DAYS YOU'RE *the hydrant.* My auntie Lindie told me that one when I was young. A student in my freshman high school class pulled my hair. So I pulled hers back. I was the one that the teacher saw and the only one who got in trouble. Both my mother and auntie had things to say about that, but when it came down to what my punishment would be back home, my mom told me to keep my hands to myself unless detention was worth it. My auntie said detention was always worth it and then she gave me that wise line about dogs and hydrants. That day I got in trouble I was the hydrant.

Today, I'm in that bitch of a position again.

"One thing after the other," I whisper into my coffee.

The steam flows around my cheeks. The sinful smell of caffeine addiction is the only thing that's been comforting so far today.

My desk chair groans as I lean back in it, staring at the plaque to the left of my door then the framed news article beside it. My JD and a story about the first case I ever won, which was published in the town's paper. Six years ago I had so much more energy than I do now.

My laptop is closed and I just simply can't find the stamina to open it again. Instead, I find myself wishing I'd just stayed in bed all day and never answered my phone.

As a sigh leaves me, I chance a sip of coffee. It's still too hot, but not scalding like it was when Aaron first brought it in. The shade of brown matches my walnut desk and I find myself smiling over the color of the coffee. I suppose in rough days it helps to be grateful for the little things. And then I catch sight of the bruise on my hand. The same shade as the grain in the desk. *So long, gratitude. See you whenever I find that thing called patience.*

Ignoring the bruise, I turn my attention to the case file laying open on my desk and read the first bit for what's now the fourth time since I first sat in here. The constant ticking of the clock seems so loud today that I stare at it rather than the black and white words and inwardly curse myself.

I never should have gotten out of bed. I never should have answered my phone to deal with my mother. I sure as hell would have made it to the curb on time to move my car so I wouldn't have gotten that ticket. If I hadn't seen the ticket as I was getting into the car, I wouldn't have slammed my hand in the door. And, most importantly, if

I wasn't pissed off and in pain, I wouldn't have said what I said to the press when I was walking into the building.

I shouldn't have said it and I shouldn't have gotten out of bed. Tension twists my gut. It's bad; today is a really, really bad day.

Pinching the bridge of my nose, I do everything I can to calm myself down. To pretend like my boss isn't going to walk in here and chew my ass out any minute now.

The parking garage is just across the street. Our building lies between an office complex and small commercial strip. The coffee shop is all the way on the other side, which is a six-minute walk, tried and true. So when I parked with fifteen minutes to spare and a hand that was throbbing just as hard as the headache my mother gave me, I knew I needed coffee.

What I didn't need was the press waiting for anyone from the Assistant Attorney General's department so they could ask questions about a case that slipped through my fingers.

Microphones and camera crews first thing in the morning get my adrenaline going in a way I used to crave. I can even admit that back when I first moved here, I loved the sight of them. The high of knowing information and having a voice that mattered meant so much to me. The fact that I worked on cases that were worthy of press was enough to keep a soft professional smile on my lips and a confident gleam in my eye as I strode along confidently with my simple black leather purse kept tight to my side. I paired a power walk with red lipstick and a skirt suit worth more than my first car.

I thought I had it all back then. This morning though,

and lately with the way the press has turned, it was hard enough to keep my lips pressed into a thin red line. Lipstick courage or not, I sure as hell had better things to do with my time than be battered with questions about a conviction that's been overruled.

I barely had a hand in the case. I gave my opinion and that was all.

"Anyone who helps a man do that to children, to little girls who were dead the moment he set their sights on them... a man who helps and does nothing to stop them deserves to rot in hell."

Needless to say, I didn't get my coffee. So I'm stuck here with Aaron's choice of brew. Which is too hot to drink still and every second that passes, the headache gets worse.

My statement plays back in my head followed by the ticking of the incessant clock.

And then suddenly there's a loud bang at my door. The *knock, knock, knock* hardly registers before the door is swung open.

"You said, 'rot in hell.'" Claire Eastings mocks my tone as she swings the door closed behind her with a hard thump from the bottom of one of her flats. She stands taller than me without heels, and that's saying something. Six feet tall and sixty years old, she towers over my desk with a scowl. Another thing Auntie Lindie used to say, *your face will get stuck like that.* ... Yeah, well, Claire's face is in a constant scowl. Despite her resting bitch face and all, she's damn good at what she does. So when she repeats, "rot in hell," drawing out the words with her dark brown eyes wide and full of disbelief, one hand on her wide hip with the other gripping a piece of paper so tight that she's creased and crinkled it, my stomach drops.

My fingers nervously pick at the edge of the case file as I meet her gaze. I have a lot to learn. I'll be the first to admit it. "I'm sorry; I shouldn't have said it."

"No," she agrees then throws her head back and when she does I close my eyes, wishing the ground would swallow me up. I don't react well to being scolded and especially not by someone I admire. Claire paved the way for women in this career, simply by being the best of the best. *Today isn't just a bad day,* I think as I swallow the knot in my throat, *it's an awful day.*

I know what I did. I know I messed up. Just tell me whether or not I'm going to have to sit out on cases and file paperwork as punishment. I have shit to do.

With my jaw clenched tight, I keep the words there at the back of my throat and give Claire's rant the full attention she wants.

Her pencil skirt isn't fitted and it rides up, bunching around her hips as she paces. "Are you kidding me?" she questions, her head tilted and her eyes narrowed at me. When she does that, the wrinkles around her eyes and her pursed lips deepen.

"First the mess that happened two days ago and now this? Are you—" She continues her tyrannical rage and I cut her off.

"What happened two days ago didn't come out of my mouth." Jill earns another dart thrown at her in my imaginary poster of her on the wall in my head. "That was a reporter trying to stay relevant."

"Well, this morning, 'rot in hell' certainly came out of yours."

"I apologize," I say and my sincerity is there when I meet her gaze, refusing to break it even though I'm burning up inside.

"Is it because of what was said? Is it because Jill said you're becoming infamous for serial murder cases going cold? Is that why you had to give your two cents this morning about Ross Brass?"

"You and I both know he did it." As I speak, the emotion that creeps into my voice, cracking it, is something I didn't count on. I know Claire hired me over seasoned lawyers well worth their weight because I'm hard; I keep my emotions in check. That's what she said. I have a hard edge and the emotion rarely gets to me. It's evidence and precedence and getting to the point.

Emotion is a weakness to be exploited and preyed upon in this business. I don't know if it's my family issues or the case from five years ago, but today is hard. I'm struggling to remain unaffected.

"He played a part in four girls dying and he got off on a technicality." I answer her as best I can without letting my voice crack again. It would be easy if all of this really was as simple as dogs and hydrants, but that's not the world I live in. I chose a career with higher stakes and things that truly matter to me.

Sympathy isn't something I anticipated. So when Claire's gaze softens and she takes a seat in the leather wingback across from me, I'm truly surprised.

"Of course he did. But when the evidence is tainted while it's in police custody..." she trails off then inhales slowly and shakes her head, shifting her curly auburn hair around her shoulders. With her hands thrown up in defeat, she adds, "It's on the PD for the way they handled the evidence. Not on us."

Leaning forward, I look my boss in the eye and remind her who she hired and who I am. "It's bullshit that they mishandled evidence and now Brass gets to walk." Taking in a deep breath, I make it known that I have more to say. "He does deserve to rot in hell, but I never should have said that to anyone other than you and our partners. I am sorry," I add emphasis to the last statement, my voice firm and then sit back in my seat. "I shouldn't have said it. Now I know why you say you don't talk to press after six p.m."

"If you aren't on point . . ." she begins and I finish her line for her, ". . . then don't say shit."

Claire's an early riser and gets into the office before everyone else. Claire practically lives at work and handles the press above everyone else, unless it's past 6:00. That's her cutoff. Now I know my limit: No coffee, no talking.

"I think my new rule should be no press before coffee." My muttered statement as I run my hand along the back of my neck forces a small laugh from Claire. If it can even be called a laugh since the sound is just a tad longer than a huff. Her smile lasts though, thank God.

"Are you pulling me off my cases?" I ask her and she shakes her head.

"No, but I will be giving you the cold shoulder in front of Tanner and Shaw. I can't let them think you got off easy." They're new to the prosecution team. Shaw used to handle defense and Tanner is fresh out of law school.

"I was serious when I asked you if Jill bringing up that case got to you," Claire states although it's meant to be a question.

Eating up time by hiding behind a sip of coffee, I deny the stomach drop and the pounding in my veins. "I'm fine," I answer her and then give her a tight smile followed by a distraction. "My mother called this morning, I got a ticket, and I smashed my hand in the door." Holding up my hand as evidence, Claire winces.

"All before coffee?"

With a nod and a click of my tongue, I answer, "Without a single sip."

Within half an hour, she's out the door, my coffee is gone and all of it goes to the back of my mind as I force myself to actually get work done and make today productive at the very least.

Time slips by as I catch up on a case that goes to trial next week. I'll be looking over Tanner's shoulder and he'll be pissed because of it, but it should be an open-and-shut case. The evidence is damning. It would take one hell of a defense or one hell of a fuckup for Tanner to lose this one.

I was so wrapped up in it that I didn't see the missed call from my mother. There's not a chance in hell I'm calling her back until I talk to Cadence. They got into it again.

If Cadence implied that she dates men who hit her because of what we saw when we were children, then my sister crossed a line. And that's exactly what my mother said she told her. I'm not her psychiatrist, but I don't understand why she'd say that. Mom said Cadence was drunk, but I just can't see that and it was hard enough to decipher it all through my mother's tears.

Intent on getting a cup of coffee from Brew House down the block, I head off, checking my phone and noting that my question to her from this morning asking if she's okay has gone unanswered.

I have two more cases to prepare for and one of them is first-degree murder.

This … tension between my mother and my sister can wait until tonight. That thought is what's on my mind when I'm aware of the familiar prick. The feeling like someone's watching me. The same one I felt last night. A glance over my shoulder proves no one's there as I pass under the awning of a bookstore. That doesn't change my gut feeling though and that fear lingers the entire walk down the block.

I make it there in under four minutes, the insecurity forcing my pace to be fast enough to get my heart racing.

Ordering the flavor of the day with cream and sugar, two of each, I convince myself it's just the case being mentioned. The case from five years ago has never left me.

It should have stayed in the past. It *did* stay in the past. One little blonde reporter with a camera behind her can't bring back ghosts long dead.

I slip the change the barista gives me into the glass jar for tips and listen to it clink as she thanks me and then I make that decision firm—the case is long over with and long gone—and that decision is not to be overturned.

The cold case is dead and there's no one watching me. All the confidence of that statement vanishes about halfway back to the office, when I swear I feel eyes on me again.

chapter
three

Cody

I KNOW THERE'S A PILE OF LETTERS IN THAT locked file cabinet by my feet. Creased from the mail and some crumpled from anger, they stare at me from beyond the thin old metal that keeps them locked away.

What haunts me isn't the past when they were first mailed to me, it's the fact that I got another today. A crisp new letter to join the others.

How long has it been since I last knew *he* existed? Years, I know, but almost five years ago I sent him one after the next and our tenuous relationship became one sided. For a year, we exchanged information. He stopped returning the letters, he stopped giving me hints that started as a taunt and changed into a mutual decision of execution.

Rumors on the street suggested he hadn't died. When

the letters stopped, I had nothing left to go on but the fear of kids and a name people spoke of as if they were naming the devil.

A part of me wished it had all ended, but a piece of me that's far too truthful, too primitive and brutal knew one day he'd reach out again.

One day the story we started would pick back up ... I simply don't know how it will end.

The metal goes *thunk* when I kick it, staring at the old dent in the side. The memory flashes in front of my eyes, prompted by the sound. A vision of me kicking the cabinet that held the only pieces of Marcus I had when he didn't respond.

For days. For weeks. Months passed with no word as the case went cold and I lost it. But hadn't I lost everything long before then? Who was I to feel anything at all but relief when Marcus stopped interfering, stopped taunting me, stopped the long-held conversation we had between right and wrong and who was next on the list.

Whiskey licks my lips and the empty glass on my desk suggests that thoughts of the angel of death serial killer will beg me to fill the glass to the brim once again.

I've picked apart the letter, every word and the unique cadence in his writing. I used to think his poetic nature meant he felt highly of himself. But when I realized who he really was, everything made so much more sense.

Knock, knock, knock, the door bangs in time with a friendly rap.

"Yeah?" I question.

"We're going to Bar 44, you coming?" Steve's voice is boisterous. As far as everyone else knows, the case is still cold. They don't know there's been another murder with the same MO.

I can't give them one letter without letting on about the others. And in those, I'm just as guilty as he was. *Not in the beginning. Not until I realized...*

"Be there right behind you. Just wrapping up something," I call through the door. Feeling far too sober than I'd like, but grateful that I haven't reverted back to the raving lunatic I felt like years ago when Marcus left me all alone to dwell on what we'd done.

Steven is off with an "all right, see you soon," and it doesn't take me long to follow. Getting ahold of myself and convincing myself that this letter doesn't change anything.

After all, there are no bodies. No list of names that he's given me.

There isn't even a riddle.

He only gave me a simple message and it's one I agree with. *Ghosts come back and I wish they didn't. He started again.*

Maybe he's gotten as lonely as I have. Maybe he's simply using me again. Although I can't blame my part on him.

A deep inhale then a slow exhale makes my chest rise and fall before I take off my jacket and change shirts to go out to the bar tonight, all while pretending those letters don't exist.

What would they do if they knew?

What would she do? The beautiful woman with deep eyes and a smile she holds just for me, what would she do if she knew I played a part in a case that nearly destroyed her before her career had truly begun?

The thoughts plague me the entire walk to the bar. Even the drum of laughter as I open the heavy doors doesn't stop it.

She wouldn't look at me like she does if she knew. I'm far too aware. Far too stung by the truth that she'd see me as a monster if only the letters were in her hands and not mine.

She'd hate me. I let him get away with his bidding and she would hate me more for it.

The certainty greets me at the same time as she does, with her beautiful smile that makes her high cheekbones appear even more feminine. Her tawny gaze and gentle sway of her delicate shoulders let me know she's more than a few glasses deep.

"Hard day," she says and her excuse comes with an air of ease and flirtation before I can suggest a damn thing. Her smile doesn't falter and the blush in her skin is hot against her sable skin. With the flowing lines of her slim-fitting, cream button-down tucked into her dark blue jeans, no one would deny that she's beautiful.

How someone so soft, so elegant and sweet came into this profession, I'll never know. It's like Marcus sent her to me. The thought makes me close my eyes, lowering and tilting my head in search for the waitress.

Whiskey will be my lover tonight.

"It's been a week since I've seen you." There's an accusation hidden in her tone which is harder now, lacking the flirtation she greeted me with.

"Just busy, promise I'm not cheating on you." The words fly from my mouth without conscious consent as I glance up at her and those wide eyes blink rapidly, her thick lashes fluttering as if surprised, as if maybe she made up what I've just said in her mind.

I'm such a prick for leading her on. But damn do I love to be wanted by her. To be so obviously desired, it makes me feel in ways I've never felt before.

Thankfully Sandy interrupts the moment and I order my go-to Jack and Coke, although I don't actually have to say the words. I simply nod when she asks, "The usual?"

"So," I say and my gaze is drawn to Delilah's slender fingers slipping around the base of her wineglass. The pale wine is fragrant, drifting to me and mixing with the sweet smell of whatever lotion she must use. "A case hit my desk today," she starts and my hackles rise, prepared for whatever case it is to be the ghost that Marcus referred to. "The evidence is unreal, and I'm bored as hell. He's an idiot for not taking the plea."

Delilah's discontent with not being challenged with work always brings a light to my eyes, a fire deep inside of me that blazes hot to tease her, to provoke her in ways I doubt any man has before.

"Is that the case with … what's his name?"

"Tanner. Yes. It's too easy to be fun." She throws back the last bit of her glass and before I can stop her, the waitress stealing my attention for just a moment with the glass hitting the high-top table, she's reaching for the thick red jacket dangling from the back of her chair.

"I've already had enough so I'm going to—"

My hand acts of its own accord, my fingers gripping around her slender wrist. My skin brushing against hers is hot to the touch, singeing and I'm quick to take it back, but Delilah stands there, still and caught in the shadow of what happened for only a split second.

My heart hammers, my pulse quickening although I don't show it like she does. I can hide my desire so easily. I'm a bastard for even thinking about getting lost with her tonight.

I've seen this vulnerable woman standing only inches from me hide everything in the courtroom. I've seen her strong and vibrant but in front of me now, in a room full of people, the lights dimmed but the intention illuminated, she waits for me. She questions everything and I can so clearly see it.

"Right," I say, my own needs protesting against the ease with which I sit back and the calmness in my tone. "Good luck with the trial, don't fall asleep in there." I leave her with a joke that doesn't bring an ounce of humor to her eyes. Even though my gaze lands on the amber liquid as I bring the heavy glass up to my lips for a swig, the corners of her plump lips dropping are clearly seen in my periphery.

I don't know what's gotten into me. For years I've sat with temptation, joked with her and confided in her. The heat between us and the sexual tension is constant, but acting on it with all we've been through together would be wrong on so many levels.

"When are you going to take me home, Cody?" she says as her small hands land on the table. She leans forward, bringing a drift of her perfume and with a single glance, a peek down her blouse, exposing the smooth curves of her chest. The gold necklace she's wearing dangles between her cleavage, swaying until I lift my gaze, staring back at hers that's drowning in need and query.

I part my lips to answer her but she stands up straight,

never breaking my gaze as she pulls her red wool coat around her shoulders and slips her black purse gracefully over her shoulder until it lands at her hip. She doesn't back down. She's never been so blatant, never been so clear as to what she wants.

"You want me to take you home?" I question her feigned innocence, but take another drink after. Alcohol and bad decisions taint the air between us.

"I had a really horrible week and I want someone to take me home," she admits to me, teasingly even, taking her eyes from mine only to pretend to glance around the room for a suitable fuck.

Anger simmers with jealousy, but my own need and greed are far more prevalent.

"We've been friends for a while, Agent Walsh. Is that all we are? Just friends?"

The way her strength leaves her, the rawness and slight suffering that are evident in her pinched brow and tightened cords in her neck as she swallows, beg me to tell her the truth.

That I've wanted her from the first time I saw her.

chapter four

Marcus

I T'S COLDER IN THE EVENING, BITTER COLD. OF all the places we've been, I love this one the most. Lincoln Park is only miles away and I still remember the first time I saw her there. Going over the details of the crime, searching for answers everyone else couldn't find. She doesn't know how close she got and if it's up to me she never will. She doesn't need to be involved.

Cody Walsh though… I think if only she pushed, she'd be able to pull out every dark secret the man has. Just like tonight.

The wind brushes against my neck, leaving a pricking sensation that I tell myself has nothing to do with the way she provocatively leaned into him back at the bar. My gaze moves from the reflection of the moon against the windowpane to the soft curve of her back as she arches. His lips barely leave her skin... not even to breathe.

That's the way I'd do it too.

Cars drive by and I don't bother to look at them. I know they can't see me here, motionless and bathed in the shadows from Delilah's apartment building. She doesn't know a damn thing about me; maybe she thinks she does, but she doesn't. I know plenty about her, though.

Specifically, that she initially requested a different floor of this apartment building, even though this one was the only one with a vacancy on such short notice. I'm surprised she stayed and didn't transfer apartments as soon as another came available. I waited for that transition, for the challenge of following wherever she went. The workaholic never made herself a priority. Maybe I shouldn't have been so surprised by it all.

But she does that to me more than anyone else. She surprises me.

Her head falls back, her lips parting and her hair laying across her shoulders then over her back as she moves. The repetitive motion is seductive, and Walsh is very much under her spell.

Her gasps aren't heard through the double-paned windows, the gap in the curtain providing my view, but I swear I can hear her still. When her nails run along his back, right before she grips onto his shoulders, I practically feel what it would be like.

Arousal is primitive, obsession demeaning... what she is... is something hypnotizing. It was curiosity at first, then respect, and now... Well, now I'm not certain what she is to me. To us and to what we started so long ago.

With the fire lit behind them, it's the only light I have with the exception of a table lamp that casts beautiful shadows down Delilah's dark skin. Her nipples pebble and just as I'm enjoying them, Walsh takes them for himself. Devouring her flesh as he thrusts into her and forces her to hold on to him.

He's good to her and I recognize that, but it doesn't, not for a single moment, mean that I'll sit back while he plays.

We had an unspoken deal. "Had" being the operative word.

I now have something I truly desire and no reason not to take it.

chapter
five

Delilah

A S MY SHOULDERS LOWER WITH A LONG exhale, I rub my right one, still sore from a horrible night of sleep. My gaze never leaves the open case file on my desk. I've been staring at it for hours.

Certain lines on the paper are difficult to read as some cases are, but this one is different. Really, they're difficult to digest.

My mother's denials and my sister's concerns ring in my ears as I read the evidence. Everyone knew what was happening, but no one did anything.

How many times he beat her, where he chose to hit her. It's all documented now, but before last week, neighbors and family all took notice, and that was it. So many neighbors said they knew what was going on. Not a single one called. They didn't think it would go that far. The woman never said anything either.

With a tight throat and a rapid pulse, I swallow and put my pen to the paper, to the exact attempt we should charge him for.

Repeated abuse isn't evidence of malice aforethought. The choices are first-degree or second-degree murder. I have to make that decision. It's difficult to determine which one we can prove when every paragraph I read is minimized by the memories brought back up so recently. The sound of the slaps and then a cacophony of painful cries that are enough to keep two girls awake in bed together, staring at the door and pretending not to cry because Mom said it was all right.

I lean back in my seat and pinch the bridge of my nose, refusing to let my personal bias affect work. The air has been different this past week and a half. Something inside of me is different and I don't like it.

I'm better than this. I've grown so much and there's no reason I can't take on this case. With a sip of coffee and a deep breath in paired with a longer breath out to calm my sympathetic nervous system—as my counselor sister taught me—I repeat my mantra until I can start from the beginning again. This time I grab a pen and travel along the pages with it to keep track, circling keywords and then scribble on a pad of paper. It's not quite a pros and cons sheet with that sharp black line down the middle of the lined paper. It's a first-degree or second-degree murder charge. Which has enough evidence to thoroughly convince a jury.

I'd focus on something else, anything else, but this

needs to be submitted by the end of the day and the only other place my mind takes me is to a few nights ago when I lost myself to Cody Walsh.

Closing my eyes, I can still feel him, the sweet lingering pain of a good fuck even though it's been days. That's all he left me with, though.

I woke up to a slight hangover and an empty bed. If it wasn't for the throbbing between my legs, I'd have thought it was only a dirty dream about a coworker.

Fuck, what did I do?

My attention is so far off from what I need that I shove both the case file and the pad of paper to the left and decide to go for a walk, to clear my head instead.

I haven't seen Cody since that night. I haven't spoken to him either. A deep pain settles inside my chest, digging there and planting seeds of insecurity and doubt.

The insecurity that stands with me as I head to the other side of my office makes me think it's all a childish crush. It was most likely a one-time thing. He may even think it's a mistake. I wouldn't know, since he hasn't spoken to me.

I barely ever dated my entire life. I dated one guy in college for a few months and that shitty experience was enough to convince me to focus on my studies. I had a fuck buddy, though. And then another in law school. It was exactly what I needed. I focused on my work and there was someone around for the release when either of us needed it.

The thought of Cody being just a fuck buddy sends a sharp pain straight through my chest, one I don't expect.

I've always struggled when it comes to men. *I suppose*

I have my father to thank for that, I think bitterly as I slip on my red wool coat and cinch it tight around my waist. My sister would argue it's our mother I should blame.

The wool strap digs into my palms as I pull the belt even tighter, staring at one article on the wall and then the next, the light from the large window behind my desk shining against the pristine glass.

Nostalgia lingers for a moment, back to the moment I started hanging the articles. I focused on putting monsters behind bars and got the hell out of our Podunk town in upstate New York.

I was so proud of this office. I thought I'd really made it and it would only get better. I thought *I* would only get better.

The door swings open without an invitation and Claire stares at my desk for a moment, her tall figure draped in a brown twill pantsuit. The expression on her face is foreboding but loses its strength when she takes in an empty desk.

"Right here," I speak up, squaring my shoulders and giving her a questioning look in return to her stricken expression.

"Did you see this?" Her voice is lowered and it's only after she hands me the paper that she turns away from me to shut the door to my office. It's not a loud bang, it's gentle. Nerves prick at the back of my neck as the rolled newspaper crinkles open between my fingers.

Claire Eastings is never gentle.

"Fuck," I mutter as I scan the article.

"'Fuck' is right. They're having a goddamn field day." Claire's comments are accompanied by her pacing back and forth in her short heels, muted from the modern woven carpet until she steps on the hardwood flooring. Then back onto the carpet and so on and so forth.

That rug is the single piece in this room that differs from the rest of the offices. Everyone else has framed photos like me, although mine are articles. Everyone else has the same black leather stationery set on a mahogany desk and an entire wall lined with bookshelves filled with necessary reference texts.

My coat is the only splash of life and color in this place. Disappointment carries to my lips, pulling them down as I refuse to read any more of the article.

"I'm not surprised," Claire comments with her arms crossed as she stands in front of me, her pacing momentarily paused. "You opened the door for criticism."

She's referring to my unfortunate "rot in hell" experience, mentioned in the article ... *twice*. "I know," I answer her with a heavy breath and suddenly my rendezvous with Agent Walsh doesn't seem to matter anymore.

"He walked, there's no proof if we can't use the evidence," I say and frustration coats every word. "Ross Brass got off. The press will fade. It's not going to trial. It's done."

"It should have been done. The press can keep it alive and compare to any other case they want." It surprises me that she's letting it get to her.

"Do you want me to issue a statement?" I offer, feeling that insecurity creep up my spine. "I can't be blamed for the PD's errors."

"No, no ..." Unfolding her arms, Claire looks past me and her gaze seems far away. There's no anger, no fire blazing there. Defeat wades in the depths of her irises. It sends a chill down my spine.

Clearing my throat, I question her, "What is it that you want me to do? How are we handling this?" Although my voice is strong and I'm able to stand tall, crossing my arms at my belly and still gripping the paper, I feel anything but when Claire looks me in the eyes again.

"Someone's looking into your background. We were alerted to the files being opened, including cold cases."

Chills flow down my arms and I stand there breathless, expertly maintaining my composure.

"You can't believe the press—" I didn't read it all, but the first line suggests that I'm either incompetent or mishandling cases. I have no doubt that the journalist is good friends with Jill Brown.

"That report is nothing but the product of a wild imagination and a witch hunt," Claire says confidently, cutting me off.

"Exactly." Stress pushes down my shoulders as I respond. "They can just say whatever they want and we ... what?"

She nods, continuing before I can make my own guess. "We assume someone is doing an exposé on a member of the Assistant Attorney General's office. A member with an impeccable record, but whatever ghosts you're hiding, I think you should prepare for them to come to light."

"Is there really nothing else they have to write about? Especially given that I've closed how many cases? My reputation is solid and one of the best on this team."

"It's not just work," Claire says then looks behind me at the two picture frames on my desk. "They will turn over every rock."

"I don't have anything to hide." A tingling heat spreads over my skin, denying what I said. But I don't have anything to hide. "I haven't done anything wrong. I've never mishandled anything."

"I know. We can't have that here."

A bitter vein of offense laces my voice when I answer her, "I'm aware of that. They can write whatever article they'd like. They can drag me through the dirt. It'll last for a moment until I win a trial and another. Or until they have something more interesting to write about."

The cords in Claire's thin neck tighten as she swallows. "Is there anything at all that they would find, Delilah? I'm asking as a friend."

Hearing my boss call me by my first name is …. unsettling. The defenses I'd thrown up crumble at the tip-top and my composure slips for just a moment, the tiredness pulling my gaze down and the pain in my back and shoulders creeping to the surface.

"Being the enemy of the press is a vulnerable place to be," she warns and when our gazes meet in the silence of the office, other than the ticking of the clock and my own racing heartbeat, she adds, "I should know."

"There's nothing for them to find. I've had a boring life and I've done everything by the book."

Claire looks away, nodding. "Well then, it will be a boring piece and they won't be able to find anything. Maybe there will be no article."

No article. Please, God, no article.

"Right," I answer and that seems to be when Claire finally notices I'm in my coat. The thick fabric makes me feel that much hotter under her scrutiny.

"Early lunch?" she questions.

"Just need another coffee," I comment and inwardly scold myself for lying. If only she picked up the thin cardboard cup on my desk, she'd know just how full it was.

chapter
six

Delilah

"**H**AVE A GOOD NIGHT THEN," I SAY AND lift my glass in salute as Aaron leaves the high table in the corner of the bar, giving me a short wave before he slips the leather jacket around his broad shoulders and heads for the door for a smoke.

"You too, Jones," he answers but I barely hear him over the chatter in the packed place. It's busy for a Saturday night and I focus on every face except for his. Every single one, taking them in, watching the way they speak, some of them a little too close as they whisper, some laughing so loud and genuinely that wrinkles form around their eyes.

I take them in like I took in the evidence of the case this morning, distracted and not seeing it at all.

Because Cody Walsh is right there, not even ten feet

from me and he's been there all night, but he hasn't spared me a glance.

His phone has eaten up most of his attention and right now he's having what looks to be a very interesting conversation with someone I'm unfamiliar with. He's avoiding me. It's plain as day. He hasn't looked at me once. He doesn't seem to have any intention of doing so either. *What a prick.* Sleeping with him was a mistake. A grave one for my ego but nonetheless, one that's over. We're nothing more than a man and a woman working closely together in a professional setting. Not a damn thing else as far as I'm concerned.

Wine... back to my wine I go because I desperately don't like feeling that twist in my stomach and the tightness at the back of my throat.

Just a sip, and only two glasses tonight. I couldn't focus at the office, so tonight will consist of sitting cross-legged on my bed with paperwork in front of me until I have every piece of evidence in line for the perfect prosecution.

Work is my comfort place and working will get me through whatever these emotions are that I'm warring with inside right now.

Trial is a dance. The steps are all taken carefully and meticulously to get to the twists and turns that wow and convince the room. It's more than a back and forth of questions, there's intention, there's a necessity in every move and every angle. Even the wording of the questions is vital. Being able to focus and pivot is even more important.

I won't sleep tonight until I know the pace and presentation that will be the most alluring and convincing. Some call the courtroom a circus, but that's just a show for entertainment and distraction. I treat every courtroom like a ballet, with a spotlight on the details. Every single detail brought to light with a pirouette given enough time and pause to show the depth of what it means.

With a glimmer of confidence, I take another sip of my wine. Aaron and I went over the basics and in only hours I will figure out exactly how we nail this prick with first-degree murder and nothing else.

"Jones." Patterson's voice startles me, but not so much that I show it. Giving him a professional smile, I offer the experienced man a nod in greeting.

"How are you doing tonight?" he asks, but doesn't give me a moment to respond before adding, "I heard you got a whopper of a case."

A whopper. Patterson's from somewhere in the Midwest, I think. Maybe he wants to know details, I'm not sure. But he should know better than to think I'd give him any. He's a defense attorney and none of his clients have anything to do with any of mine. So this is … peculiar.

"You know how it is," I answer him with a shrug that brings his attention to my blush-colored blouse. But not to my shoulders. His gaze dips lower and the heat of embarrassment creeps up my chest. "When you have a series of plea bargains and boring cases, you get hit with a difficult one to throw you off." Setting my wineglass on the table and pushing it away slightly, I add, "Can't have too many easy ones, can we?"

Patterson looks between the glass, my chest, and my face. The slight sway in his stance and the red in his cheeks betray any air of being sober the man has. He's simply had too much to drink.

"That's true," he comments, pointing at me with the hand he's also using to hold his whiskey. The ice tinks on the glass. My father's a whiskey drinker. Never on the rocks though. He said the ice melts and weakens it.

The thought reminds me that Patterson is old enough to be my father and rich enough to buy him four times over.

Patterson seats himself, occupying the chair Aaron recently left empty. "You know when I worked with your father years ago, he used to say the same thing."

My father was a lawyer decades ago. Pride wore on his face the day I told him I was going to law school. I'll never forget that day. But his career was incredibly short-lived. The lifestyle, he told me, simply didn't suit him and Mom wanted to move back home.

"Is that why he gave it up? It was too easy for him? Or are the stocks just paying better?" Patterson questions me.

I shrug again and this time when Patterson's gaze drops, I lift my glass of wine to block what little of my cleavage could possibly show from that angle.

"My mom wanted to move back home," I answer straight-faced. We never wanted for anything and grew up in a nice enough area. It may have been a small town and not anything like New York City, but we were well-off. Maybe not as well-off as Patterson; I have no idea. "I'm sure he would have stayed had he known what the firm would become," I offer him with a polite smile and a nod of recognition.

There's a murmur of agreement from Patterson and then he takes a swig of his drink. I look away, not wanting to continue the conversation.

Patterson knows far more than I do about my father's departure. I'm not privy to my parents' decisions back then. And I don't like to have conversations involving sensitive topics knowing I'm lacking relevant details on said topic.

"You know I was surprised you came down here of all places." Patterson doesn't quit, leaning back in his seat. "I get it, wanting to stay on the case and transfer..." he pauses and nods, dropping his head. "That's commitment," he comments into his lap and raising his brow, which forms a series of lines on his forehead.

"I was just starting and took it as a sign."

"What's that?" he questions, not following and I don't know if it's because of the whiskey or because, like my mother said, it was crazy that I was moving to stay with a case.

"The firm was a starting point so when the offer came up and evidence led us here, it seemed like a sign. Like I was meant to get into federal criminal law."

"And what did your father think of that?" Patterson questions. "I'm sure he was able to help you. He has strings to pull. But to help you go into federal criminal law..." he trails off and makes a face just then. One I'd like to punch but instead I simply smile.

My father and him were defense attorneys. "Working for the prosecution shocked him, but my involvement and dedication didn't." I give him the same answer I gave Claire five years ago. And just like her, he nods with understanding.

"You certainly worked your ass off to get here."

The smile on my face is genuine as I say, "And I appreciate the help I got along the way."

His asymmetric smile widens and he lifts his glass to

me in cheers, but just after taking my sip, Patterson's smile fades.

Before I can turn to my left to look at whatever's taken his attention, a heavy arm rests across my shoulder and Cody Walsh kisses my cheek.

I barely catch sight of him before his lips brush against my skin.

What the fuck is he thinking? My heart spasms as I smile like it's a joke and push against his muscular chest, which barely moves.

"Do you have a minute?" Cody questions, his brow furrowed as he ignores Patterson. The older man is up from his seat and leaving before I can hiss at Cody, "What the hell are you thinking?"

Adrenaline races through me as I tuck a loose strand of hair behind my ear, the long day wearing on the simple bun I'd styled my hair into this morning, and casually glance around the bar.

Aaron saw what Cody did, that I'm sure of. He has the decency to look away when I catch him staring.

Shit. Shit, shit, shit. It will be the talk of the office. As if I need any more buzz around my personal life and intentions right now.

"I'm sorry I didn't come over sooner; I've been busy." He speaks as if it's a given. Like he was genuinely busy. Does he think I'm a fool? I have eyes and common fucking sense. He was ignoring me and we both know it. I'm not an idiot and I don't like being treated like one.

"What the hell are you doing, Walsh?"

"Saving your ass. He was eyeing you up and you didn't like it. I know damn well you didn't."

"He's my father's age and my father's friend." The excuse doesn't dissipate Cody's scowl; it only makes it deepen. And quite frankly, I second-guess myself at the term "friend."

"Don't lie to me," Cody reprimands me. He has some damn nerve.

I grit my teeth, laying cash down at the bar for the glasses of wine and grab my coat. "You have some fucking nerve to come over here pretending to be a knight in shining armor when you've ignored me for days." The last word is practically spit out of my mouth.

I could choke on emotion right now, but I'm damn good at ignoring it and better yet, at hiding it. I give Cody the cold shoulder and silence as I make my way out of the bar, but the stubborn fool follows me.

Shaking my head and huffing out a sarcastic breath, I turn to look at him as the entrance doors close and a gust of wind blows against my bare neck.

"I don't have time for a man who doesn't know what he wants." My anger is palpable. I don't know what gets to me more. Him ignoring me after sleeping with me, or him affecting the way colleagues see me by implying we have a romantic relationship in the bar.

I don't care to figure it out. Not here in the cold night on the corner of Main and Spruce.

"I'm already up shit creek with the press. I was fine with having something low key. But ignoring me? No, I didn't sleep with you because I thought you'd treat me like I didn't exist after. And I sure as hell didn't want it out in the open. I get it, you don't want a relationship, but causing a scene isn't my style. I don't need any more prying into my life," I mutter under my breath and push Cody back another step.

"I'm not prying."

"No, you're kissing me in front of everyone after leaving without a word and not speaking to me for days."

"You needed him to back off," Cody says, keeping up his hero mentality and it only pisses me off more. Is he not hearing me?

"Is that what you were really doing? Saving me?" I practically hiss. The weight of the other night lays on my shoulders. I glance around to make sure no one's out here, but even in the empty street, I feel the familiar prick. It's an uneasy sensation, only adding to my annoyance and frustration. "I want to get out of here."

"Because I kissed your cheek?" Cody asks as if it's an insult and I take it as my cue to cross the street. Holding my coat tightly closed and ignoring Cody behind me as I walk as quickly as I can to the garage.

"Don't follow me."

"Don't leave then," Cody responds.

Why does it have to be messy? Why couldn't this have been low key and easy? The same at work as it's always been and if we needed each other, we'd act on it. That's what I thought it would be. Just as I figured Cody would, he follows me as I storm off toward the garage, my irritation growing with every step. Both with myself and more so with Cody.

It's not until I get to the entrance of the garage, standing just before the concrete stairs that will take me to my car that I ask him, "When did I become a damsel in distress? Not once have you walked me home. Not one goddamn time!" The spite in my voice surprises us both. The hurt in my chest lingers and I struggle with what I've just said.

"I would have taken you home if you'd asked."

"I didn't and I'm not now," I answer, turning away from the hurtful look in his pale blue gaze.

"Why are you so pissed?" he asks. "I'm sorry I kissed you in there. I get it. You want this to be low key and—"

"This?" I say, cutting him off, not hiding my shock and irritation. "What is *this*, Cody? Because you slept with me, which I initiated, I take that on, I get that. But then you left without a word and ignored me repeatedly. It would have been fine if it went back to normal. So what exactly is *this*?"

"I don't know," he says and his demeanor changes, like he's struggling between remaining a guarded wall or giving me a look like he's a wounded puppy dog. If he wasn't so handsome, it would be pathetic. But as it stands, the look makes it difficult to stay angry.

"You don't know and I don't know either, but you don't get to make a public statement because I fucked you one time. My career is more important to me. The way they see me in there matters," I say and throw my hand up, pointing at where the bar is down the street. "What the hell were you thinking?"

"I fucked up. I'm sorry."

I don't know how to respond, so I cross my arms, letting his apology sink in. I'm grateful for it, but damn am I hurt and still pissed, even if that emotion is waning.

"I don't know how to do this, but I want to talk."

Now he wants to talk? "Not tonight; I have to work. I had a shit couple of days. I just need to go home."

"Then let me take you home," Cody offers, ever the gentleman and I can at least respect that but I'm not exactly ready to just let it all go. I can't just let it go. Ignoring me, ghosting me, and then getting all touchy-feely with me in the bar? He could have handled this any other way than how he did. I suppose I could have too, but I'm too tired, too overwhelmed, and too pissed off to think about it right now.

"I can take myself. I'm fine." The bitter note in *fine* is the cherry on top of this shitty night. I shake out my hands, trying to let it all go before digging in my purse for my keys.

"I know you're still mad. I'm good at pissing people off."

The confession tumbles out of me before I can stop it. "I wonder if you'd have even come over to me if someone else hadn't hit on me." *Shit.* It hurts to say it out loud. I could have left and he wouldn't have even said hello to me if someone else wasn't scouting out his territory. My hands go clammy. It would have been easier to just ignore him and go about my night. *Why the hell did I let him get to me? Why did I go after him when I knew it wasn't going to work?*

"That's bullshit," he says and his conviction makes me doubt myself.

Lifting the strap to my purse higher up on my shoulder, the keys still not found, I question him, "How would I know? You didn't message me. You couldn't even look at me. Was it really that bad?" I'm proud that my voice doesn't break out loud like it does in my head. "No one likes to be ignored. Especially not by a man I just slept with this past weekend."

"Don't do that," he says. Cody's voice is comforting but I don't fall for it.

"I'm not your problem, so I can do anything I want, Agent Walsh." I'm close to turning away from him when he takes my elbow in his grasp and before I can object, places something in my hand.

"I was texting you this," he says and closes his hand around mine, forcing me to take his phone. "Just read it. All right?"

"I don't want to read a text when you could have sent it and didn't." My annoyance does nothing but fuel him to stare me down until I let out a frustrated sigh.

"Just read it."

Finally, I look down at the phone, if for no other reason than to appease him enough to let me leave. The bright screen lights up and I see he's brought up his messages between the two of us. It's a long message that he's referring to, one left unsent. I have to scroll up and when I do, I accidentally hit send. Shit. I guess it doesn't matter if I'm reading it anyway. Letting out a slow breath and ignoring the squeal of tires from someone leaving on the opposite side of the mostly vacant garage, I start to read the message Cody thinks is going to change my mind.

I enjoyed last night.

That's the first line and I don't get much farther. "It wasn't last night," I comment, letting my head fall to the side and seeing for the very first time in years, a vulnerable Cody Walsh.

With the lights from the parking garage illuminating his face, he looks younger than I've seen him before and my breath slips out easier as I remember his hard body over mine, his muscles flexing as he took me, pressing my back against the sofa and rocking himself into me ever so slowly but deeply to bring me closer to my own release before he found his.

"I didn't start writing it today," he admits, scratching the back of his neck. His five o'clock shadow combined with that boyish smirk makes me warm to him.

Dropping his phone back in his hand, I don't read the rest of the message.

"I enjoyed it. I like you. I just don't know how to not fuck it up."

"Going caveman isn't something I'm interested in," I offer him.

"You want this to be discreet?" he asks and I simply nod.

"Read the rest," he presses, pushing the phone toward me but I reject it. Only the phone; I don't reject him. My heels click on the pavement as I close the space between us and tell him, "I sent it to myself so I'll read it when I get home." With a nod and a simper, I add, "Maybe I'll text you back before the week is up." It's only a lighthearted joke and it does exactly what I want it to. Cody relaxes his arms around me, letting his hands fall to the small of my back. I'm tall in my heels, but he's still an inch or two taller than me so he has to lower his head to whisper against my lips, "Don't be mad at me." His plea isn't lost, but neither is my frustration.

"Don't ignore me ... and don't kiss me in public," I say and the statement isn't spoken harshly. Maybe there's even a small plea hidden in the gentleness with which I spoke it.

As I close my eyes, I know I shouldn't be doing this. I

should end it between us. My life is complicated enough. It felt so good though and I've wanted him for far too long to throw it away. Even when all the warning signs are flashing bright red lights in front of my face.

He pulls back just slightly, his inhale making his chest rise and I find my fingers itching to slip up his jacket and lay right there against his white t-shirt that's taut against his skin.

"Is this public?" he questions, his voice laced with desire and his pale blue eyes simmering when I lift mine to his.

As I part my lips to answer him, he captures them in his, stealing my response and my breath just the same.

Tilting my head and rising up just slightly on my heels, I meet his need with my own. His hands play against my back, keeping me to him and my own reach around his neck, loving the skin-on-skin contact and wanting more of it. Needing more of it.

As his tongue melds with mine, the heat of our embrace enveloping around the two of us, I wish I could get lost in his touch tonight.

But I can't. My eyes open before his and I pull away, breathlessly and with a heat rolling through my body. Cody stays perfectly still a second longer than me and takes his time opening them. His steely blues stare me down with the look of a hunter. A look that makes me feel so very much as though I'm his prey.

"Not tonight, Agent Walsh," I tell him with my heels steady on the ground and he grins at me before stepping forward and planting the smallest of kisses on my jaw, his strong fingers brushing against my neck and hardening my nipples with the simple touch.

He catches that my eyes close when he kisses me. I know he does from the look of triumph on his handsome face.

"Drive safe, Delilah."

It's not until I get home that I read his text.

I enjoyed last night. I enjoyed you.

I don't do flings and I don't do girlfriends.

I don't fuck around with coworkers or people I see day to day.

You know I don't have time for a relationship. I've failed at every one of them I've ever had. I'm going to fuck this up. If this is even a thing. If this is something that you want to do again.

That doesn't change that I want you. I've wanted you for a long damn time and even after last night, I want you still. I can't offer you commitment and I'm not good at much of anything other than my job.

That's where his message stopped and I'm quick to respond before I think too much about anything he said in this text and focus only on that kiss under the lights in the parking garage.

Don't think about it, just take me home tomorrow night.

chapter seven

Delilah

EVEN WITH THE CURTAINS CLOSED, THE SUN creeps in, waking me from a much-needed deep sleep. My eyes are heavy at first, but my body is so relaxed and at ease. The blush comforter, two shades lighter than the matching curtains, slips down my body as I sit up, stretching and note that the side of my bed Cody slept on last night is empty. I can't help but to touch it and when I do I find it's cold.

He left already.

He's good at that. We leave separately from the bar, and meet back here. At least we have the last two weeks. Thus the relaxed muscles and deep sleeps. A good fuck is a miracle worker for the tired mind and sore body.

Letting out an ungodly long yawn, I stare down the

paperwork that litters the top of my dresser. I worked magic in this apartment to give it a mature, fresh and feminine feel. A place I could hide away and forget all the bullshit and hardness of my day job. Who was I kidding? Every surface of the bright white furniture is covered with evidence of what I do. The fact is, I bring my job home. Always. It's not about being a workaholic; it's simply that I can't let go of things that matter.

There's a memory for every inch of this room. Moments when haunting evidence seemed to unveil a truth to me in the late hours when I couldn't sleep.

I can make this room as pretty as a page out of a home décor magazine and it still wouldn't matter.

The silk sheets rustle as I get up and that's when I see the note on the bedside table between the alarm clock blinking 12:00 in bright red. In other words, someone in the unit tripped the fuse again. With a frustrated exhale, I check my cell phone for the time and fix the clock before reading the note Cody scribbled out for me.

Going to New York for a case. I'll miss you.

Two sentences are all he wrote, but the last one leaves a smile on my face.

Opening the drawer, I slip it inside with the two others he left me.

The first:

I'm sorry about the last few days, but not about the part in your bed. Call me whenever you want. Or text. I'll be waiting and I'll try not to kiss you whenever some prick eye fucks you at the bar. And yes... I meant it when I said you look sexy with that silk scarf in your hair.

The second one he left is inconsequential, like this one,

but I keep it anyway because it makes me smile. Nothing has changed at work between us and there haven't been any other incidents. If Aaron or anyone else suspects we're seeing each other, they keep it out of the gossiped conversations in the break room. Or at least they haven't had the nerve to confront me.

My bare feet pad on the floor and I wrap the belt to my thin cotton peach robe with cream lace tight around my waist as I make my way to the kitchen. Today's my first day off in … Lord knows how long. Coffee and then I promised myself I'd relax. Truly take a moment and read or maybe I could take my sister out to get our nails done. It'll be a little over an hour drive for each of us, there's a shopping mall halfway between us. It's perfect for our get-togethers. She's barely spoken to me since our last call. We've had our ups and downs but of everyone in this world she's my rock. Only a year and four days apart, we've gone through life together. Everything that's happened, every milestone and pitfall.

We fought like cats and dogs in high school and I even have a faint scar on my face from one spat where she scratched me. College came and we drifted apart for a moment; the photos on my fridge are proof of the distance. So many pictures of when we were children, then nothing of us together until I was a junior in college and her a sophomore. I went for a law degree, following my father's path. My sister went for psychology. We studied together, partied together. We were each other's wingwoman in every way. My mother always said we'd be best of friends and that we needed to rely on each other. It's odd for her to say that considering her falling-out with our aunt, but she was right.

Ever since college, we don't go long without a call between us. It's been nearly two weeks, the longest that I can remember, and the realization makes my empty stomach sink. I've been too preoccupied with Cody and work.

Pressing the brew button and listening to the water heat up in the coffee machine, I write out a quick text to her:

Off today and tomorrow. When are you free to meet up?

After I press send, a deep crease finds itself in the center of my forehead. I have twelve unread messages and two missed calls. Both of them from Claire. No voicemail left.

Swallowing thickly, I go through each of the messages.

I'm so sorry.

They're such assholes.

Are you okay?

You need to call me.

The texts vary from coworkers to family members. I'm confused about most of them, not writing back a response until I know what the hell is going on.

A text from Aaron includes a link to an article. Written by Jill Brown's associate. The opening paragraph makes my jaw drop and it's then that the coffee machine sputters, announcing the hot cup of coffee is ready.

As if a cup of coffee could fix this.

I wondered what they'd write about and of course I'd give these assholes ammunition to keep the negative press running.

With my fingers going numb, I read the entire article in record time, feeling the anger rage inside of me. They bring up my father and his old cases, which is infuriating. His career has nothing to do with mine.

Worse, they bring up my relationship with Agent Walsh. Questioning if either of us were fit for the case given our romantic relationship. As if we were in one back then.

Can Miss Jones's judgment be clear while pursuing a romantic relationship on the field? The first case that went cold was with him and since then a series of murder investigations have led to no arrests. Those cases are worked by both the woman in question and Cody Walsh of the FBI.

I feel fucking sick to my stomach. Dropping the phone to the counter, both of my elbows hit the granite and I bury my head in my hands.

My father's integrity as a lawyer has never been questioned. Oddly enough, Patterson isn't mentioned and I wonder if he had a heads-up on the story. If maybe he even leaked the information about Cody and me.

Rubbing what little sleep remains from my eyes, I process everything again, breaking it down bit by bit in between swigs of coffee. Claire is going to be pissed. She's going to be furious.

But the facts remain the same: they're running a story because I've been notable recently, even if in the past there were a number of cases that ended up going cold. A pissed-off criminal lawyer, fairly inexperienced and working for the Assistant Attorney General... they were given one comment I made on the street and they ran with it, letting imagination get in the way of facts.

Internally, I prepare my response to Claire.

I didn't make the press by losing cases. The media has focused on the fact that so many of my cases don't have enough evidence to even go to trial. Cases that they plaster everywhere and then demand justice. They want someone behind bars. All the cases are murder investigations. At least the ones mentioned in the article are and those are the ones that require me to work with Walsh. Mostly against crime organizations that are established and difficult to penetrate.

They aren't the only cases that matter, but they bring in the most headlines, and higher ratings on the news.

They want someone to pay, and they thought going after my family's history in murder trials and my romantic relationship would paint me as a villain. As someone incapable of performing her job. Worse still, they question my intentions for this position. The last lines of the article imply I have ulterior motives. That I don't want the cases to go to trial because like my father, I'm protecting murderers, the mob, and serial killers.

With shaking hands, I reach for my phone, desperate to get in touch with Walsh. This is bullshit. I've never been so angry in my life.

I worked tirelessly to get here. I've dedicated every waking hour to pursuing the same assholes they want to see locked up. It's one thing to not be good enough, it's another to have your intentions questioned.

As I hit the call button, two things happen at once.

I get an email from Claire that I read while I place the call on speaker, listening to the ringing:

We're issuing this statement in response to the article and you have a mandatory one-week paid leave while we investigate. Lay low, and stay out of the press.

See the attached document.

Investigation? Really? I don't expect to feel betrayal, but I do. The attached document is a defense for me but it's short. I don't know what else I could expect. The statement is merely them covering their ass.

The second thing that happens at that same time is that my sister texts me.

As I read the text, Walsh's voicemail greets me when he doesn't answer and I don't have the presence of mind to hang up. I'm lost in what my sister wrote more than any of this bullshit. Dread sinks down to the soles of my feet and anchors me there in that moment.

Mom's in the ER. You need to come home.

chapter eight

Delilah

Just let it pass. Cody's text is a single line. His answer to my extremely long voicemail is a single line.

Hours go by before he texts again, hours of driving through the mountains of Pennsylvania and up to the Podunk town in New York where I grew up.

I'm at a gas station before he messages again: *This break will be good for you. Your mom needs you and by the time you get back, all of this political bullshit will have passed.*

My stomach stirs with the faint smell of gas and the whirl of cars driving down the worn asphalt road beside the gas station. Staring up at the faded sign, I do what I've always done—I breathe through it all, not letting it get to

My mom's arm is broken. She's not sick or dying. I won't be here for long and then I'm going home to look into that journalist. With my message sent, I slip the phone into the cup holder and finish up at the gas station.

Regarding the article, I'm pissed, Cody seemingly couldn't care less.

When my phone rings at the swinging red light to get back on the interstate, I nearly answer it until I see it's my sister. I'm pissed at her too. My heart fucking stopped when I saw her message about our mother.

I didn't even know it was only her arm until I was half-way here.

She wouldn't answer; neither would Dad.

Anger swarms inside of me. Coupled with disappointment and resentment. Could anything else go wrong this week?

Some days are harder than others in the career I've chosen and it took me a long time to realize it's like that with family too. Some days … some days I just wish they would be honest. I still would have come. I know Cadence would argue that I wouldn't have, but I had the time off and I didn't need to be manipulated into coming back home.

That's exactly what it feels like and my discontent with my sister is why I drive the rest of the way, nearly two hours, without the radio on and my phone on silent. I didn't even realize it until I parked in the hospital lot that I hadn't turned the volume back up. Sometimes a person just needs quiet.

A few hours of quiet to clear my head and let Cody's suggestion sink in: *Just let it pass.*

I can do that, I think as I climb out of the car, my purse hanging from the crook of my arm and the light jacket I threw on before leaving not doing a damn bit of good up here where it's colder. At least I can try, but I can't stop caring.

Absently, I nudge the door shut with my hip, cradling the bouquet of flowers I picked up for my mother in my arms. As I walk into the small hospital, I can't recollect what I even packed. It was a furious effort to gather up my luggage and leave immediately.

I asked my sister what happened. She said she didn't know.

It's a difficult task not to set my jaw into a straight line when I see her as the glass double doors open and the visitor section to the left of the desk is visible. *Mom could've been dead. I thought she was dying. How could she let me think the worst and not answer me when I demanded to know more?* The words pile on top of each other in the back of my throat when I see my sister, but she doesn't see. She doesn't see any of the resentment, any of my anger through her blurred vision.

I nearly tumble back when my sister, slightly taller than me, skinnier and frailer in every way, wraps her arms around me and sobs in the crook of my neck.

I'd hold her back but I can't move my arms; she's gripping me so tight and my hands are full.

The anxiousness and fear sink back into my blood, slowly coursing through me.

"It's just her arm," I whisper to my sister in a dual effort to comfort her and also remind myself. "It's just her arm, isn't it?"

Cadence is slow to unwrap her delicate self from my

body. She should've been a model, I swear. As she does, I take in the scene behind her. Auntie Susan is in the waiting area too. My God, I barely even recognized her. I don't see Dad anywhere. The only other people in here include the woman working behind the desk and a man with his son in the opposite corner of the waiting area. There are only two rows of seats on the right side of the entrance. But we have our own corner it appears, judging by the two coats spilling over one chair and where Auntie has her purse on the coffee table next to two cups of what I know is tea. None of the women in my family drink coffee but me.

My gaze is brought back to Cadence when she sniffs and wipes her eyes, apologizing with that hint of shame for breaking down. Steadying her with a grip on her forearm, I ask her, "Where's Dad?" The rustling of the plastic around the flowers is all I get in response because Cadence breaks down again, silently crying and walking off to gather a tissue.

Hitching my purse up my shoulder and straightening my coat, I take my time making my way to my auntie.

I set the flowers and my purse down on the end of the coffee table and take off my coat, laying it on the third seat from the end. My auntie in the corner, then my sister, then me.

"Hi Auntie," I greet her, stepping in front of my sister to lean down and give my auntie a hug. I expect it to be brief but she holds on to me tight, whispering that she's glad I'm here before she releases me.

Her tone is tense and that's what keeps me from asking the question again: *it's just her arm, isn't it?* Dread is a difficult thing to swallow; even more difficult to talk through.

"Dad's talking to the police." My sister speaks up before the silence passes too long. Her slender fingers run under her eyes gracefully before wiping the mascara that mars the tip of her fingers on her black skinny jeans. I know my sister very well, and she simply threw on those clothes. Yet, she still looks beautiful. Her hair in curls, her face fresh and bright eyed. She's wearing a chunky cream knit sweater that hangs just low enough to show her chest and the cream against her light brown skin complements her perfectly.

Even with tears in her eyes, she's beautiful. And she looks just like Mom. Everyone used to say it growing up; her skin is lighter than Mom's, but that's the only difference between them. She got our mother's femininity, and I got our father's intellect and ruthlessness.

"Why?" I question, crossing my ankles and observing, taking everything in. "What happened that he has to talk to the police?"

My auntie looks off in the distance, staring at the worn mural on the far wall. It's nothing special, a mundane piece of art displaying trees and a sunrise made of tiny mosaic tiles. Something to comfort people and do nothing more. My auntie stares blankly at it while my sister stares at me, her hand landing on my forearm.

"She broke her arm; she said she fell. But the other bruises are older and she has a number of fractures." My sister whispers the last sentence, swallowing harshly as she lets the implication hang in the air.

My first thought is that it's been a long time since they've fought. We were children back then and he never touched her like that after. How awful is it, that

73

I know even as my chest goes tight and my fingers cold, that he's hit her before and yet I don't want to believe the accusation.

"Did he hit her?" I ask outright. How the question comes out evenly, I don't know. I can feel them both staring at me, their eyes boring holes into the side of my face as I stare at the steel elevator doors, wishing a doctor would come down and say I could see my mother, so I can ask her, rather than sitting here with people who don't know. They don't know. Mom would tell me. She'd tell me the truth. They had their problems early on, but they're over. She broke her arm, that's all.

Dad wouldn't do that; he wouldn't hit her. My mother is a strong woman. She wouldn't let him. This is all a mistake. Isn't it? It's just a misunderstanding.

Fuck, I think as I drop my head and close my tired eyes. My mind's playing tricks on me and my emotions are storming inside of me, whipping me around until I can't think straight.

"Did he hit her?" I repeat myself, louder this time when neither of them answers. Auntie doesn't say a damn thing, but she doesn't stay silent either. She's deliberate when she grabs one of the two cups off the table in front of us and makes her way around the other side of it, saying she'll give us space.

It took me a long time to realize the reason for the tension between my auntie and my father.

He came from money, had a white-collar job. He was powerful, older and white, marrying a younger black woman from a poorer neighborhood. "Trophy wife" was a term used a lot when we were younger.

My mother once screamed at her family that they couldn't be happy for her. That they hated him because he wasn't like the rest of them.

I thought she was right because my grandmother, her mother, never did seem to like him. But then again, my father's mother never seemed to like my mother. It went both ways. All of my grandparents died before I was ten and I hardly remember them but I do remember the way they looked at their child's spouse. Like they didn't belong together in any way.

I thought my auntie had the same ideas as my grandmother.

Until Mom left him one day, taking us to Auntie Susan's and both of her sisters told her she needed to leave him. I was too young to realize what was going on. Cadence knew before I did. She's younger, but she remembers far more than I do. That was the one and only time, though.

"I wouldn't be surprised if he did," my sister finally speaks, her voice lowered and careful. "They haven't been getting along recently."

"Well, what did Mom say?" I question her, feeling my pulse strike harder. I struggle with the way my sister sees my father. I know they had fights, they had bad moments, but there were so many good ones. So many times they kissed each other in front of us. So many happy memories and occasions that were pure joy. What they went through before was a rough patch. That's what my mom said, it's what she called it, a *rough patch*.

"I want to know what really happened," I comment and as I do, I feel warm tears at the corners of my eyes.

"I think I started it," Cadence whispers in a choked voice then reaches for her tea. She holds on to it like it'll protect her, her shoulders hunched inward. "I called Mom because... that guy I was with. He was rough the other night and I don't know why, I called her and I blamed her." Her voice cracks as she slumps back into her seat.

"What?" Disbelief runs rampant through me. Unpacking everything takes time, but the first reaction I have is to protect her, to defend her from whatever fucker she's referring to. "What do you mean he was rough with you?"

"He just pushed me against the wall. I told him to leave when we got into a fight over something stupid. I don't even remember."

"Who is he?" I ask and my voice is deathly low.

"No one now. I'm done with him. I blocked him and he's not interested in me anymore anyway. Not after what I said to him."

I can only nod once before waiting for her to continue.

"I was upset and I called Mom and told her and she was so... so judgmental." The hurt is there in her voice, but so is guilt. It's riddled with it between each quickly taken breath. "So uppity about him and what happened and all I could think is that it happened to her and she stayed with him.

"And I went off on her... I said some things I shouldn't have."

"You think she got into it with Dad afterward?"

"I don't know for sure, but ... I just ..."

With one arm wrapped around my sister's shoulders, I pull her into me and let her rest there as her face contorts and she cries again.

"Have you talked to Mom?" I ask her and she shakes her head. "It's been hours," I remark.

It takes my sister a long moment to respond, "She was unconscious."

There are four nurses in the corner of the hospital cafeteria. And then there's my auntie with a plate she hasn't touched, and myself. I move the mac and cheese around with my fork, in the same situation as my auntie. Not wanting to eat, but not ready to leave just yet.

My mother seemed fine, apart from her arm wrapped in a cast.

She smiled, she gave me a kiss. She said it got stuck in the railing when she tripped. She was trying to hold on to it and instead she only made it worse.

If it wasn't for the look on my father's face, I'd believe her. He got her two vases of daisies, her favorite flower. The smell of them in the hospital room haunts that moment for me. Three vases total, one bouquet from me, lining the room and bearing witness to that conversation.

I can't be in the room with them. I don't know how my sister's doing it. How she can sit there with speculation but not say anything.

"How's the city life?" Auntie Susan asks me and I bring my amber gaze up to meet hers. It falls quickly to her gray sweatshirt with the block letters from my uncle's alma mater. He passed a few years ago, a car accident caused by black ice.

"It's not like New York City."

There's a hum of understanding as she stirs a pack of sugar into a steaming cup of tea. Her dark eyes watch the swizzle stick as she asks, "You like it better down there? I bet it's warmer."

"It is. It's ten degrees colder here every time I come up."

The small talk doesn't do anything to help the hollow feeling in my chest. Or the numb prick along my arms. I want to talk to someone, but words fail me. That and shame. I don't want it to be true, but my gut is hardly ever wrong.

"You know what I told your mama?" my auntie Susan speaks up, and the bluntness of it forces me to meet her gaze. "I told her when she went back to him, that I was always there for her. If she wanted to come stay, if she needed money. I told her if she wanted a family dinner, I'd sit next to him but not in his house. I would never step foot in that man's house."

Hate seeps into her words, her disgust showing through and the first crack in her armor showing. My auntie's frame is larger, not at all delicate like my mother's. She shifts her weight and corrects her expression before continuing, hardening her disposition.

"We make choices, and your mother made hers. Your father made his. I make my own too. I'm not leaving her, but you can't make sense of it with your mother."

I don't speak. Not to her. Not to my sister. Not even to my mother.

I'm silent as I take it all in. Collecting the bits of evidence and forming my own conclusion. I feel dead inside. There's this pit in my stomach that's cold and unforgiving.

My mother says it was an accident and that's all there is to it as far everyone else outside this room is concerned.

I leave before everyone else and without telling them. The last thing I want is to be alone with my father. I don't want him to look me in the eyes and lie to me. Worse, I don't want to believe him when I feel so certain that he assaulted my mother and should be behind bars right now.

Flowers are waiting for me at the hotel desk when I check in. I wish they made me smile, but they're so much more beautiful than daisies. That's all I can think.

They're the first thing I see and that smell… the smell fills the entire room. Tossing the keys onto the dresser and letting my purse and the luggage bag sit at the front of the room, I make my way to them.

My fingertips trail down the deep red petals, the smell of the roses covering up the memory of the daisies. A dozen deep red roses.

After washing my face and changing into sweats, I text Cody: *You didn't have to send flowers. But they're beautiful.*

His first text hits me like an ice bath washing down my bare skin. *I miss you and I've been thinking of you, but I didn't get you flowers.*

A follow-up text from him does nothing to help: *Now I wish I had.*

He's the only one who knew I was staying in this hotel. I only told Cody because he asked if I was staying with my parents and I told him, I always stay here.

My limbs are shaky as I move to the window of the hotel room. I'm on the second floor so there's no reason I should see anyone there, but still, I look over every inch and then do a search in the room, checking in the closet, in the bathroom. I search every inch and then lock the door before heading back to the roses. There's no note. No indication of who they're from and the clerk at the desk said she didn't know. They were simply left here specifically for me when I checked in.

A dozen red roses that keep me up most of the night until I slip into a light sleep, filled with brutal memories.

chapter
nine

Delilah

THREE DAYS IN MY HOMETOWN IS PLENTY.
Add in two family dinners with forced smiles
and my mother doing her best to tell us she's fine
and everything's all right, and I couldn't wait to leave.
I spent every moment I could in the hotel providing lies
about how much I was needed at work.

There was only one moment I was alone with my father and he called me out on that lie subtly. All he mentioned was the article and he told me the same thing that everyone else did: it'll pass.

He didn't say a word about Mom. He didn't let on that it was obvious there was tension between us. He knows I think he hit her. He knows everyone thinks it.

But in that moment at the restaurant when everyone

left and I had to go back for the to-go box of leftovers I'd forgotten, he didn't mention a damn thing but the article when I ran into him scribbling on the receipt at the table.

Three days of feeling insignificant and like I'm only playing a part in a poorly written film. Four times I tried to reason with my mother, coaxing her to tell me the truth when we were alone. All four times she denied anything had happened other than her being careless. Even when I stared at the other bruises. I've never seen a sad smile on my mother's face until I said I was leaving. I'm just not sure what she's most sorry about.

I need to see you. My text to Cody remains unsent even though he's back in town and so am I. But we haven't seen each other. I spent two days at home before forcing my way back into the office at work.

Claire only agreed because I promised I had no intention of doing anything but paperwork.

There's always plenty of that to do, was her answer.

It wasn't a yes and it wasn't a no. So here I stand, in my office staring between the piles of cases that need to be sorted and filed electronically and my empty cup of coffee. Aaron is technically in charge of these tasks, but I'm grateful to simply be doing something and he's grateful for the help.

If I told a younger version of myself who thrived on working in the field that I'd be hiding behind files in a silent office for days on end because of PR pressure … I would have snorted the most disbelieving laugh followed by a quick, "Fucking hell I will."

Reality is a bitter pill to swallow sometimes.

The rap of a quick knock at the door is a pleasant distraction. "It's open."

Claire's gaze moves from me to the stack of folders over a foot high and the open cardboard filing box. "You busy?" As she asks, her smile quirks up and her left brow raises comically.

"I think I need another coffee before I dive into the next stack," I comment offhandedly. "You have something for me?"

At my question, she makes her way into my office, closing the door behind her with a soft click.

"Just checking on you."

With my head down, moving several folders from one pile to the next, I peek up at her and her dark gray skirt suit before answering. "I don't need checking on."

"Of course you do." My motion pauses in the air, a manila folder in my clutches before she adds, "We all do."

I've been an honor roll student, salutatorian, and been given every kind of overachiever trophy a person can be awarded. I don't like the idea of being someone who needs to be "checked up on."

"I'm good. Almost through with this stack and then it'll be ready for Aaron to put in the system and be digital." My statement is practically robotic if not for the dismissive tone.

Crossing her arms, Claire leans back, one heel up and braced against the closed door. "Shaw is clumsy and Tanner struggles to read the jury."

The huff that comes from my lips brings a smirk with it when she adds, "They're too green and I want a string of cases to go our way. I might've managed an article with the *Journal* but it's on hold until we have a series of verdicts go our way."

"Running defense?" I question her, hating that she spent any time at all to combat the article that ran last week.

"I'm doing what has to be done. We need you in there."

Silence weighs heavy on my shoulders. I can't remember the last time I went this long without preparing to go before a judge. I haven't even gone to Bar 44 or seen anyone other than Aaron and Claire since the article hit.

"Everyone goes through it," Claire speaks up as if reading my mind. "Shake it off and meet me in the boardroom. I'm not giving this case to one of them to fuck up. Nail it and we'll ring it out for all it's worth. As far as I'm concerned, the investigation has been conducted and we found nothing."

"What are we looking at? Case wise?"

"Double homicide," she says. Her answer is spoken easily enough and with the glimmer of a challenge in her eyes, a fire lights inside of me.

This is why I do what I do. I put the bad men behind bars. Some people claim we're only here to show the evidence. That there's no desire or intention to punish.

Fuck that.

"You need this," Claire claims and I nod.

"I need it more than you know." I let the truth slip out firmer than I would have liked.

"How's your mother?" Her question comes with an assumption that I need the case as a distraction. She's not wrong.

"She'll be all right. Just tumbled down the stairs and hurt herself pretty bad." Even to my own ears, the statement is spoken without any emotion. Inside, turmoil spreads, disgust even because I don't tell her what I really think. Sucking in a breath and letting it out in one go, I stare down at my boss in her typical professional attire and tell her I'll be there, abruptly ending the conversation.

I'm busy making sure I put the files back in the correct boxes and email an update to those who need it when Cody messages me.

I need you tonight.

That's when I see the message I never sent him, still waiting: *I need to see you.*

I change it to: *I want to see you too, but I have a lot of work and probably won't go to Bar 44.*

Even though the three moving bubbles make me aware that he's writing something in response, I quickly add: *But I need you too.* There's a vulnerability I don't like in my words, so I lighten it by adding a joke: *Come to my place? Make it a quickie?*

I can't explain why I feel sick to my stomach over it. Or why unease spreads through me until he responds, *It's a date.*

chapter
ten

Delilah

"I HEARD YOU MIGHT BE LEAVING TOWN FOR A while." My voice carries a purr to it as the bottle of beer hits the high-top table. It's nearly 2:00 a.m. and the bar's clearing out.

A week of normalcy does wonders. No one's brought up the article and as far as I'm concerned, it never existed.

"Bad news travels fast, doesn't it?" Cody's formerly charming expression dims under the bar lights. Office, trial, Bar 44, and bed with Cody. Every day on repeat.

"I thought you were going home?"

"I am," he answers, tipping back his drink.

"Going home is bad for you?" The disbelief in my voice makes me feel like a hypocrite and Cody's amused expression displays the sentiment.

"I don't really have a home anymore. And I never liked that town to begin with."

There's something sobering I didn't know about Cody. It's easy to get along with the man, easier to get in bed with him. But getting information out of him is something far more difficult. I consult my wineglass, giving him a moment before questioning more. "Your parents?"

"They passed when I was younger. I went to live with my uncle who never wanted kids and he has dementia now." He shrugs, but nothing he said is casual in the least.

"Sorry to hear that," I respond apologetically and brush my thigh against his, leaning closer to him even though I know the bar is hardly packed.

"I hate his dementia. Hate going to see him even if I love the man. He was more like a friend than a father. And now…"

"He doesn't remember you?" The question tumbles out of me with pain and it's relieved when he shakes his head and answers, "He remembers me. He knows who I am most of the time.

"It's just … he asks about things that happened before. He forgets about my parents passing. He thinks I'm my father sometimes. And then others he remembers. It's hard to tell what reality he's in and what I'm going to get when I visit him."

It's quiet for a moment and I want to tell him I'm sorry again but it seems not good enough. They're just words and I struggle to find something more than just an apology.

"He used to ask about cases. I liked that better."

"Yeah, it's easy to talk about work," I'm quick to agree with him, nodding my head even and offering a gentle smile. "If you need to vent about anything, I'm always here."

His mood shifts back to easy when he smiles and tells me, "I'm not leaving for a week, though."

The way he raises his brow makes me huff a short laugh and say, "I guess I'll just have to put up with you for a little while more then."

As I joke with him, he brushes the back of his knuckles against mine and the heat unfolds inside of me.

There's not a lot that makes me melt, but I swear he does.

"It's easy to hide in work. Even easier to hide under the sheets and get lost, forgetting who we are and what we do," Cody admits, speaking lowly, like it's a secret.

"Why do we do this?" I don't know why the question leaves me. It's not with conscious consent. I suppose it's the thought that neither of us likes to go home. We don't like to talk about anything but work. Why do we put ourselves through this? Why do we prefer to meddle in lives that are long gone and stay buried there when there's so much more to life than this?

Walsh's gaze slips lower than it should, landing between my breasts as he questions, "Do what?" The edge of the bottle rests against his bottom lip for a moment too long, forcing me to pay too much attention to his expert lips.

"Do this job," I answer firmly and holding an edge that doesn't last. With my teeth sinking into my bottom lip, I return his hungry eyes with a heat in my own.

We should stop this conversation in public. I should stop leaning so close to him.

We've gotten too comfortable and even when I glance around the place, noting that no one's watching and no one cares, I know damn well we shouldn't be reckless. Especially after that article and the insinuation made. Even if I've nailed four trials in a row, I don't need the judgment affecting my job.

"Why do we do what we do…" Cody's intonation lowers, becoming more serious as he stares at my nearly empty glass of white.

"That's what I was wondering?" My question doesn't bring his gaze back; he's lost in something reflected in the glass.

"I know I do this because of my brother." Every muscle in my body tenses. Carefully, feigning a casualness that I'm all too aware is absent from this conversation, I pick up the glass and sip the white wine after commenting, "The one who passed?"

We spent over a year working together before anyone mentioned the fact that Cody Walsh had a brother. It's one of the very few things I knew about him.

"Yeah, he's the only brother I had. He was just a kid."

"You were too, weren't you?" I question, my memory betraying me. I'm almost certain his brother was seven or eight and Cody was only ten.

"Maybe I should stop. It's been a long day and I've had too much."

I shrug nonchalantly and say, "Whatever works for you. I do love getting to know you, though."

I always knew Cody had demons. Something dark and twisted that kept him quiet and guarded whenever his personal information was in question.

The second his guard would start to crumble when I first met him, another would go up behind it, thicker and even more impenetrable. There's not much about the man's past that I know.

He's a workaholic like me. He cusses under his breath when he's pissed and likes beer on easy days. Jack and Coke when he wants to think about something that's bothering him. He always says it's a case. He lives for his job with the FBI and I get it.

My first real job was with the FBI, although not as an agent. I was only a lawyer working the cases with them. Cody was the knight in shining armor, willing to do whatever it took. Last one to call it a night and the first one to gather us in the morning.

Brutal tasks require brutal men. To this day I don't know what makes Cody the man he is, only that I want to know his secrets. I want him to trust me enough to do so.

"You don't have to stop. I want to know." Laying my forearms on the table and leaning forward so I'm closer to him, I add, "You can tell me." I'm vaguely aware of a couple nearby gathering their things and leaving. The sound of clinking from glasses being collected fades as I fall into Cody's light blue gaze.

It swirls with an intensity, but deep inside the shades of silver and cobalt are secrets locked away, rattling behind the bars where he holds them hostage.

"What happened to him? You never did tell me the story. All I know is that you two were split up and he passed a little while later."

"It was years, not a little while. I went with my uncle; he went to my aunt when our parents died." When he told me the two of them were split up, I assumed his mother and father had split. I didn't know they split after.

"That's rough," I barely speak, feeling a tingle of unease run through me. "It must be difficult to be separated like that… especially after losing your parents," I offer even though my voice is tight.

"We were never close." Cody's response isn't spoken coldly, but it strikes me still. "He was years younger than me. He was only a kid," he repeats the last statement in a whisper, finding refuge in his beer and I get the impression that the conversation has come to a halt until he speaks again, surprising me.

"It was a group of three men. They kidnapped and murdered those kids. Fed their remains to the dogs. The one who lived told the cops they had to watch it all. They saw everything happen to the kid before them. One at a time as they huddled together in the cell and were forced to watch."

"That's sadistic," I respond and I don't know how I'm able to even speak.

"They got off on scaring them," he responds and his tone is harsh.

"They got them though, right?" *Please tell me they got the bastards.*

"You could say that. They're all dead. It never went to a trial."

How did they die? The question is right there, but that's not the one I ask. "You were how old?"

"I was twelve. My brother was eight. We were split three years before."

"I'm sorry."

"One of the kids they abducted when they took my brother survived. The one who lived said my brother died only hours before the police got there."

My heart pounds in agony. "So that's why you do this?"

"Yeah," he says and pretends like he's tired, and that's why he rubs his face down with one masculine hand before looking away.

"You want to tell me your sob story now?" Cody asks and he makes fun of himself, trying to downplay it all, but I see right through him and I love what I see there.

I answer his question with one of my own, "You want to get out of here?"

chapter
eleven

Marcus

I WAS CORRECT IN MY ASSUMPTION THAT DELILAH would call the front desk and then call the local floral shop when she received the roses. Both of which would give her nothing. I was right about her not telling Walsh as well, beyond asking if they came from him.

With the pad of my thumb running down the stubble along my jaw, I wonder if she would have told him had she not been in the position she was in. If the stress of that article and her family dynamic didn't make her so tense and she was more clearheaded.

I can practically hear her laugh as the waitress gives her another glass of white wine. I'm not sure what Sandy told my Delilah, but it brings a glimmer to her gaze that's been missing for days.

It still surprises me how easily she hides so much pain behind that gorgeous smile. I lean my head back against the leather headrest, listening to the police scanner and diverting my gaze to the front of the bar as opposed to the window I can so easily see her through. For a moment I wonder if I should have sent her wine instead of roses. The smile slips across my face, the feeling unusual as I imagine her uncorking it just to dump the bottle down the drain, not knowing who it'd come from.

She would have enjoyed the smell of it, though. I've seen her inhale deeply so many times when that cork is popped from her go-to bottle of *Valley Pines* Pinot.

The leather seat groans under me as a familiar operator announces a disturbance four blocks from here. Nodding, I recognize the address and continue to hear the flow of conversations, but I'm not listening as intently as I should. Instead, my gaze moves back to Delilah as she talks to her coworker, Aaron Curtis. She doesn't know how he watches her.

She doesn't see but I do. As does Walsh.

At least the young man knows she's out of his league. He doesn't have the balls to admit he wants her. There's a small bit of gratitude I offer him from a distance. It's one thing to know Walsh takes care of that need for her. It'd be different if the man fucking her was ... so inferior.

As if it's his cue, Cody comes into view, sidling up beside her at the bar-height table. She stiffens, becoming far more serious than she's been all night. A voice alerts me that the scanner is still on, the shrill white noise of it filling the cabin of the car before I lean forward to turn it off, silencing it to keep any more interruptions from disturbing this moment. The days have turned to weeks of this. Him approaching her, the two of them pretending there's nothing between them.

The act may have fooled most of them, but Aaron knows just like I do. He saw it months ago, when they started to drift together.

Unlike Aaron, it only makes me watch more closely. I want to know what Cody says that convinces her to leave when he does, to let him meet her at her house and let him through the door.

I want to know what she whispers in his ear when he enters her late at night when they think they've gotten away with it all. When they think that no one knows that he comforts her at night.

He must know that I know. How could he not? *We had a deal.* Maybe I hadn't made myself clear enough.

Rage simmers inside of me, but it's easily subdued.

Cody Walsh had to know what he was doing by bringing her into this mess. The article was his warning. I know he read it and received the message loud and clear. Perhaps he doesn't care and he's going for her, giving in to the temptation regardless.

I'll bring up the past, then I'll bury him in the present. Even worse, I'll start the chase all over again and lure little Miss Delilah back to me.

I was so close to having her before. I wonder if she remembers.

She's still the same, even if years have passed. Still the same vivacious woman with a heat in her eyes and yet there's an innocence about her.

The vision of her is only obscured for a moment by

Cody walking around her to speak to someone else. I watch her watch him.

Her lips part slightly before she forces herself to look away.

The ache is indescribable. She could look at me that way. If things had been different, she could look at me the way she does him.

I've never wanted anything or anyone like I want her and the sick part of me knows it's because Cody pursued her. It's a jealousy I haven't been able to kick.

Still, I wanted her first. There's no way he doesn't know.

He knew I cared for her and he stayed close to her.

He knew I was watching and he fucked her.

He knew what it would do to me. Cody Walsh knows me far too well to be unaware.

Even worse, he ignored my latest letter.

Do you ever regret it? Letting that evidence slip through your fingers so you could ensure I executed a different plan of yours?

There was an unspoken deal, a bit of camaraderie between us. I'm not the one who changed things. What happens next is his fault, his doing. Not mine.

part ii

this love hurts...

chapter
twelve

Delilah

"I'D LIKE TO REMIND YOU THAT YOU'RE UNDER oath, Miss Parks." I'm aware my voice is harsh, demeaning even, as I look across the courtroom at Missy Parks' flushed expression. The sheen across her forehead and upper lip only adds to my suspicion. I think she drove the car. We don't have proof. Not a shred of evidence, so I don't hint at it; I didn't charge her with a damn thing because I wasn't certain I had enough to convince a jury. My red heels click on the shiny obsidian marble floor in Judge Partings' courtroom. I may not be able to tie her to the robbery, but her testimony is crucial to ensuring her boyfriend goes down for his part.

After all, he's the one who killed the eleven people inside the bank that night. My hunch that she was driving the car is only that, an inkling based off of years of experience. My gut instinct tells me she didn't know he was going to shoot anyone. Thus the sweat along her brow and how frequently her voice shakes, requiring her to repeatedly clear her throat.

She's an accomplice to murder and she knows it. I wonder if the guilt eats her alive at night.

"I'll ask you again, did you expect your boyfriend at the time, the defendant, Mr. Wilson, to meet you at your home that Friday evening?"

"No, I mean," she says as she shakes her head, her gaze on the floor to my right. She can't even look me in the eye and knowing that, I walk with a set pace toward her, forcing her to look at the harsh sound of my heels clacking. "He—he…"

The pencil skirt of my suit is tight as my gait widens. It's custom tailored, as is my jacket. In contrast, Missy is wearing a shirt far too large for her frame and the same could be said for her jeans. Her attire reinforces her mousy demeanor, making her appear that much more minuscule as she raises her widened eyes to me from the stand. The poor girl looks like she hasn't eaten in days and her hair pulled back in a ponytail so tight it makes my own scalp hurt, only makes her appearance look worse.

"We've gone through your whereabouts and text messages surrounding the time of the crime, Miss Parks. The defendant saw you every Friday evening." I make sure I point to him, forcing her to look back at him. *Look at him. Look at the man who you know committed murder.* I pray the jury sees how her expression displays horror just glancing at him.

"Six weekends in a row he met you at your house and stayed the duration of the weekend. After the previous Sunday, he was out of town so you wouldn't have been able to meet in person and according to your phone records there were no calls between the two of you." My voice is tight in a ruthless manner as I stare into her eyes now glossed over with unshed tears. I'm conscientious about keeping my body language nonthreatening. My tone and the way our gazes meet may be strict and unrelenting, but the jury needs to relate to me. They need to want to ask the same questions that I'm asking. I lower my voice just slightly and knit my brow as if I'm confused. "So please, enlighten me as to why you wouldn't have expected him to be at your house that evening. Because every shred of evidence points to the fact that your boyfriend should have been with you that evening."

Her bottom lip trembles as she shoves both of her hands into her lap. With her shoulders hunched she appears defeated. It would be a dream come true for her to just admit it. To admit she drove to pick him up. That they spent six weeks together planning a robbery and she's the one who drove. If only she would admit they were together... but that would be a fool's errand.

Wiping under her eyes, Missy sucks in a deep breath, her shoulders shaking as she holds back a sob. I'm quick to grab the square box of tissues and hold them up to her.

"I realize this is a difficult time, Miss Parks." She nods, greedily accepting the tissues and playing the part of a mourning woman. Someone shocked by the actions of her on-again, off-again boyfriend. But the twenty-four-year-old won't get much sympathy from this jury. It's filled with married women much older than her and the evidence of the defendant's past led to one very obvious question: why was she still with him? And the manner in which it's presented points to a conclusion: she was the one who had control over him and bailed him out, but then left him to rot when she couldn't handle it. She called the shots, at least in her relationship.

"So why wasn't he with you on the night of August fourteenth? Why didn't you expect him to be there?"

"I lied," the young woman blurts out, blinking rapidly as she looks me in the eye, tears still clinging to her lashes. Hope blooms that maybe she'll confess. She speaks clearly, "I did expect him." She nods quickly and repetitively and then speaks to the jury, not to me. "I don't know why he didn't show up and I was expecting him."

"Why lie and say you weren't?"

"I just... I didn't want to hurt his case anymore."

Anymore.

The word lingers and I allow a space of time to pass. I let it hit the jurors one by one. In my periphery I see the juror in the back row on the left, a man in an old brown suit, tilt his head, the question marring his forehead with a deep crease.

I could ask how she'd already hurt his case; I could push her more. But this dance is delicate. I have to play my part as well.

With a soft nod, one of sympathy, I announce that I have no further questions.

Let the jury think I'm inadequate by not pushing for more. After all, my gender and race already do that for some of these men and women. Let them be angry that I didn't interrogate her. That I didn't ask the obvious question. Because the implication is already there. The defendant's girlfriend knows he's guilty.

I know it. They know it. And that's what I needed from her.

Glancing at the defendant, I catch sight of his anger and more importantly the betrayal in his eyes as he stares at her, his ill-fitting black suit sagging on his slight frame. *Now he'll talk.* I'm not the only one who knows she drove. Nothing in this world is more spiteful than a scorned lover.

I make a mental note, as the nineteen-year-old holds his girlfriend's gaze for as long as he can while she exits the stand, to offer him the deal again. To give up the getaway driver in exchange for a lighter sentence.

Tapping my pen to the untouched legal pad on the table in front of me, I think, *I'm damn good at my job. If nothing else, at least I'm damn good at this.*

A familiar prick at the back of my neck follows me all the way back to my office. I offer tight smiles to everyone I pass as I make my way to the elevator, both hands on the handle of my twill briefcase. Chills flow down my shoulders, the kind that make your insides churn. Glancing over my shoulder when I feel eyes on me again, I know there's no one there, but I can't help it. I half expected to see Missy. Maybe to give me damning evidence, maybe to tell me the truth and offer to make a deal since she has to know he's going to throw her under the bus now that she's given up defending him. Goosebumps run down my arms when there isn't a soul in sight. I stare a moment longer, looking past the empty hall and toward the large bay windows.

People pass quickly, walking on their own or in pairs beyond the glass. Not a soul sits still. There's no one.

Ding. The elevator arrives, snapping me back to the here and now.

Shaking off the nerves, I keep my head in the game. Sometimes this happens. The brutality of what I deal with gets to me sometimes. The doors shut and in privacy I snag a mint from the pocket of my tailored jacket. Sucking on candy or mints helps at times. I read an article about how breathing affects the nervous system and sucking on candy is one of the ways to control breathing. I chose mints after learning about that little trick.

With the small mint on the center of my tongue, I suck, pressing it against the roof of my mouth as the doors open, once again announced with a *ding*. It's all very mundane and repetitive. Day in and day out, I do the same thing. To the office, to the courtroom and then home; or to the bar first and then home. Day in and day out. It's the way it goes and the sight before me is one I've seen time and time again. The emotions though, the charge of energy, the relief at times and the disappointment at others... there's nothing mundane about that.

Alone in my office, I quickly busy myself with writing up the proposal to present to the higher-ups regarding Winston's case. Missy's boyfriend has to know by now that the writing is on the wall. When the phone rings, I've nearly finished, but it doesn't matter.

It's Carl, Winston's lawyer. He already handed over his girlfriend and confessed everything. "Get the testimony and I'll sign off on everything then present it to the judge tomorrow."

The asymmetric smile on my lips grows to a full-on grin. I'll take my win however I can get it.

Hanging up the phone and relaxing into my chair, I check my cell phone. I've never wanted to share my victories before. Not even with my sister. She doesn't like to hear the details and it's impossible for me not to give them. But right now, I want to tell Cody. I know he'd get it. He'd understand the high of nailing both of them—that's real justice. But he'd also get the draining feeling after the adrenaline dissipates. When it all comes down and the next case hits my desk.

Dropping the phone to my desk on a stack of folders, I opt for a glass of wine from the mini fridge of my office. The small door opens and reveals there's not a damn thing in it but a half-eaten sandwich that I should probably throw out and a nearly empty bottle. I can't believe I left that small of an amount in it. It's maybe a quarter of a glass, if that.

Well damn, I think with pursed lips and kick the door to the fridge shut with a gentle nudge, the bottle in hand.

I pour it all out into a clean mug from my desk that's supposed to be used for coffee and boasts some company's logo on it. The sip is sweet and I savor it. Letting my eyes close for a minute, the moment they open I stare at my phone.

I can put away murderers and pit lovers against each other... but I can't text a man I'm sleeping with. A ridiculous huff forces me to shake my head and I down the last bit of wine; it's practically a shot.

I check our messages.

There are no new texts from him. We last spoke when he called two days ago and it was a quick conversation, but still, he called. He made that move. He showed he was interested. My inner voice tsks that I'm trying to make a pros and cons list in my head rather than having the balls to just message the man.

I could text him. I could tell him how proud I am that I got a conviction without having to rely on a fickle jury for a guilty verdict.

Still, I hesitate for one reason. I've never leaned on anyone before, simply because I don't want to. I don't want to get in the habit of having someone there, only for them to leave one day.

I'm already a little too close. A little too eager.

A knock at my door shuts down my thoughts and I set my phone aside once and for all, facedown before slipping my heels back on and answering it.

It's late now; most of the people in the office should be gone. Nearly everyone left at 6:00 for a celebratory drink I turned down to work on this plea deal. The door opens with a click as I ask, "yes?"

To no one.

No one is there and as I lean out of my office, checking left and then right down the empty hall, the chill comes back, that prickling along my neck which then flows down my arms.

It's as I'm closing the door that I see the note.

At least I think it's a note. I'm quick to pick it up and

even quicker to close the door and then lock it. The freezing cold runs through me and it's followed by confusion as I turn over the thick rectangular white paper, finding it to be blank.

What?

Swallowing thickly, my throat dry and a nervous heat coursing through me, I stare at the closed door, wondering what the hell is going on and finding myself more anxious or nervous or possibly even scared than I'd like to be.

"It's only a piece of paper," I chide myself out loud and move to toss it in the trash can along with the empty bottle of wine, but as I slip my fingers down it to throw it away, I feel a groove in the paper, an etching along the crisp page.

It takes me a moment of standing there alone in my office as the sun sets deep and low, stealing the lighter colors of the evening sunset with it, before I reach into my desk for the only pencil I have. I'm careful as I angle the tip along the one groove I feel. I follow it along the paper, listening to the ticking clock seemingly slowing down as my heartbeat picks up and I read what it says.

Breathe. I force myself to steady my breathing and double-check that the door is locked.

It wasn't a random piece of paper that was dropped, and I didn't imagine the knock I heard. I don't hesitate to call security, slamming down the buttons as I stare at the door and then below it, to the strip of light that shines through unobstructed, letting me know there's no one there. I'm still not moving from this office without security.

They answer on the first ring. "Security."

"I need an escort."

"Ma'am, are you all right?"

"No. Someone is on floor three or was a moment ago. They left a threat at my door and I need an escort as soon as possible, please." I'm vaguely aware of how calm my voice is even though inside chaos ensues.

I'm not crazy. Someone was watching me today. Someone wants me dead and I think I know who.

The man on the line tells me to stay with him and asks what the threat was. I read the note aloud. "If they rot, you rot with them."

"We have the footage from the security cameras," the detail informs me. "We'll find whoever it was." He doesn't tell me anything I don't already know, but still I nod in understanding and thank him.

The man's voice is deep but professional. It's soothing too. When he rapped his knuckles on my door and called out my name... I'm ashamed at the immediate relief I felt. I have a gun I carry too. Still, there's a lot to be said about having a trained professional by your side.

"We'll know who did this within the hour."

"I know," I say again. I've hardly spoken and I know I'm poor company at the moment. "I just want to go home right now." *And get the hell out of here.*

With his black hat on and heavy beard, I barely get a good look at Steve. He has broad shoulders though and his uniform doesn't hide that. The other one, who's waiting outside the garage, is less impressive in size. I'm far more familiar with him, though. His name's Taylor and he's been here for years.

Steve must be new; I haven't met him before. "I prefer the stairwell if—"

"I do too," I say, cutting off the newcomer, already knowing protocol. This isn't the first time I've been threatened. Although this feels different. If someone's waiting for me, the last thing I need is to have a set of doors open and reveal a gun pointed at me. Stairs all the way, my thighs be damned.

Pressing the side button, I check my phone again to see if Cody's called back as we walk up the flight of concrete stairs to the second floor where my car is parked. The sounds of the city traffic behind us reverberates in the lot as I see I have no missed calls or messages.

My throat is dry and tight with that new information. I called him the second the two men in uniform came to my door to escort me to my car, relieving the security guard who was on the phone with me.

With a deep breath in and an even deeper one out, I tell myself he must not have his phone on him. That's more comforting than the more likely scenario: he saw and judged my call to be less important than what he was already doing.

"You all right?" the man to my right asks me as I pull out my keys. There's a note of something in his voice that throws me off. It's probably only concern, but it sounds more intimate with his voice low the way it is.

A breeze whips around me and I hold my purse closer to my side, my keys in my hand. I hit the button to unlock my car, noting that it's just the two of us now; the man I trust is a floor below. The beep resonates in the garage, bouncing off the concrete walls.

"Just shaken up," I admit and try to get another look at his face, but he lowers his head as I do, so it's only his sharp blue eyes that I get a glimpse of. Only a glimpse.

For a second, I think it's Cody. A split second, but I know that's only because I want it to be him. That disappointment only adds to my discomfort.

Slipping his hands into his pockets and nodding at the ground, he answers, "Yeah, I can imagine." There's an air about him that I'm drawn to. He's intentionally keeping his distance, but there's something else. I can't put my finger on it.

Before unease can come over me fully, he turns his shoulder to me, effectively dismissing the moment, and tells me to drive safe. Taking it as my cue, I ready myself to get the hell out of here and go home. I miss my bed and the safety of those four walls.

The click to my door opening is met with the screech of wheels from someone on the street below and I glance up to see the security guard has already walked away and is standing at attention in front of the elevator. He stands with his back to it and I know that means he's waiting until I drive down to leave.

My engine turns over and I put the car into drive before I can secure my seatbelt. I want to get the hell out of here.

I don't expect Steve to step forward as my car rolls by him. With a racing heart, I slow and again I'm surprised when he offers me a folded piece of lined paper on my way down. My window's rolled up and he didn't block my way.

A part of me knows I don't have to stop. I could keep going. If I wasn't curious or I didn't want to get a better look at the man, I would have done just that. I would have kept going and gone on my way guilt free.

I don't put the car in park, but I do stop and roll down my window. I'm very much aware of the gun in my glove compartment.

"Delilah." He calls me by my first name and a pang in my chest alerts me to it. "If you need me," he says, slipping the paper through my window. With my fingers wrapped around it, he doesn't let go. His eyes are sharp with slight wrinkles around them, showing his age. Mid-forties maybe. There's a darkness that lies in the depths of his irises, and a severity in the way he looks at me. That's not what has me sucking in a sharp breath; it's the heat of his fingers as they press against mine until he lets go of the paper.

The contact is so hot, so unexpected, that I rip my gaze away from his to glance at the note in my hand. By the time I look back up, his back is to me and he takes his spot again at the elevator, not giving me a chance to respond.

Lifting my foot off the brake, I continue down to the ground floor of the garage and I don't stop until I get to the exit. My head is a whirlwind and I'm so messed up right now, that by the time I reach for my pass to slip into the meter, I've convinced myself I'm making things up in my head. The note scared me more than I'd ever admit to anyone and I just wish the man were Cody. I miss him... worse... I feel like I need him.

The arm to the gate lifts and my eyes shift from the gate to the lined paper hurriedly tossed in an empty cup holder.

Taylor nods for me to leave but I don't. I reach for the

note and it crinkles as I unwrap it to read a phone number and then a name. A name that drains the blood from my face.

The biting frost drenches me from head to toe as I read: *Sincerely, Marcus.*

Slamming the car into park and listening to the *ping, ping, ping* as I grab my gun, leaving the glove compartment open, I then leave the driver door wide open too. I run to Taylor, screaming for him to call backup. At the sight of my gun, panic flashes in his eyes.

"Backup," he says into the radio on his chest as he reaches for his gun, turning in all directions, searching for whatever's spooked me.

With my breathing coming in hard, I position myself with my back to the wall and alternate looking between the elevator and the paved road that would lead Marcus down to us.

I'm all too aware that he could escape down a stairwell on the other side of the garage. He could already be gone and more than likely is. Hiding, stalking... he's probably watching me right at this very moment.

My heart pounds as Taylor screams at me, his gun now pointed at the stairwell next to the elevator, very much catching on that someone's here.

Sirens wail in the background and I know we'll be surrounded soon.

And the man I've heard called a ghost, the grim reaper... the angel of death... he'll be long gone but he'll know my reaction.

With my throat tightening and my lungs screeching to a halt like the tires outside, I can barely breathe.

This is what true terror feels like.

Marcus is here.

He touched me.

Taylor relays the events through his walkie-talkie and several cop cars make their way past us, not stopping and heading to the next floor, searching the darkened place with flashlights.

"How well do you know that man?" I question.

"Who? Steve?"

"Yes!" I say, practically screaming like a crazy woman and feeling a burn at the back of my eyes. "Steve is a wanted suspect. He's a murderer."

"You requested him."

"What?" Disbelief colors the single syllable.

"He met me as I walked up. You requested him!"

He's the man who was never caught. The cold cases that are turning up again.

We thought he died or moved on when the evidence ran dry and the murders stopped.

Every crime scene I've been on flashes before my eyes. The blood, the faces. Vomit threatens to come up as I try to answer Taylor.

"He's a murder suspect." I barely manage to say the words as three cop cars park just outside of the exit with their lights flashing blue and red in ominous patterns.

My arms fall to my side and my knees feel like buckling as I brace myself against the wall, my defenses down.

As the doors open and close and more men stream out, their guns drawn, Taylor continues to question me. His voice berates every sense I have.

"He's the one who left the note…. he's—" *Oh my God.* I can barely breathe. He threatened me.

"No. No, they caught the kid who did it. There's footage." Blinking back the very real fears wrapping their arms around me, I take in what Taylor tells me. They found the kid, they have him in custody.

"So there are two men out for me?"

"Did Marcus threaten you? What did he do? Tell me everything."

Taylor's gaze sinks deep into mine, pleading with me and the numbness inside takes over as I clear my throat and relay everything. The odd feeling between us, the note. The signature.

"I'm going to need that, Miss Jones," states an officer I hadn't even realized was beside us, reaching for the note.

"Of course," I answer but don't hand it over just yet. "Let me take a picture first," I add. I don't wait for his response and the objection is thwarted by Taylor; he knows me too well.

With my back to the two of them and the building surrounded by men in uniform, I photograph the note and a chill comes over me. My fingers slip over the words and I note the lack of indentation, the smooth writing, the curves of each letter.

"We found something," a voice calls out from the stairwell, coming into view with the slapping of his shoes against the concrete. Staring at him, I wait with bated breath and note there's something in his hand… he carries it over to where we're standing, the red and blue lights still flashing across our faces and the stone wall behind us.

"Is it possible he was wearing this?" the cop questions. I've seen him before.

It's short, it's dark and as I close my eyes and picture

Marcus, his sharp blue eyes scold me, forcing my eyes to bolt open. He was wearing a fake beard and that's what's in the cop's hands.

"I didn't get a good look at him," I answer with my arms wrapping tighter around myself, "but yes. I think he was."

The night continues, the sounds and the flashing lights and the speculation consuming every moment but all I can think about, all I can see and feel are those pale blues and the singeing touch.

If he's not the one who left the note, how did he know to insert himself so seamlessly the way he did? Questions pile up and not a single answer comes to light.

"You need to go home. I'm taking you home." Taylor's statement comes with a hand on my shoulder that startles me back to the present.

With muted voices on his speaker and then white noise, Taylor presses the push-to-talk button and answers, "Copy that," before moving his hand to the small of my back.

"Let me drive. Andrews will follow and I'll ride back with him." With a nod and a thank you, I don't protest. I can barely think straight. I can barely even see what is directly in front of me. Instead I recall the cases. The first time I met Cody and the FBI team that was assigned when the bodies started compounding on one another.

His signature was the letters. His script matches the note. The entire quiet drive home I glance between the photo on my phone and Taylor, who does his best to comfort me, but the kindest thing he does is turn on the radio.

If he wants me dead... I'd be dead.

What the hell does Marcus want from me?

chapter thirteen

Cody

THE MESSAGES COME THROUGH ONE AFTER the other. Reception out here in this part of Virginia is a bitch and as I sit in the back of the van, I listen to each of them get worse. It's the makings of a horrific nightmare.

In the first one, Delilah disguises her fear with a sense of indignation. Knowing she's scared, my blood instantly runs cold. *Where are you?* But she ended the call with a softer, *I need you.*

She can't hide the fear in that statement.

Which makes the second and third messages harder to listen to.

Marcus.

My reaction to hearing his name on her lips is visceral.

Bastard! Anger tears through me that he went to her, that he dared to make contact with her.

I'll kill him. If he touches her, I'll cut his fucking throat open.

Attempting to play off the emotions that roll through me while surrounded by my team in the back of the van, I can barely respond.

"Right, Walsh?" Evan jokes, shoving his shoulder against mine as we head down the highway.

"Right," I say as I nod in agreement and then lean forward, gripping the back of Parker's headrest. "Hey, I need to stop up here for a minute," I call up to the driver, Bradley. The van has always seemed small with the six of us spread out in the eight-seat vehicle. Two in each row and the black cases in the back stacked up just behind me.

I do all right playing it off even though I feel sick to my stomach, and my hand's wrapped around my phone with a viselike grip.

They all know about Marcus, but they don't know the truth. The details are where the betrayal lies and they wouldn't understand that.

I don't rush out of the van when we stop. If I did, they'd know something's up. They probably already do. I don't want them involved any more than they'll insert themselves without being told shit. They only need to know what they already know about me and Delilah, which isn't a damn thing.

She's for me to take care of and unless I really need them, I'm keeping them in the dark. That's the way it has to be. The rest stop is typical. They're always the same. Gas station on one side for passenger vehicles, with diesel pumps on the other for trucks and other commercial transport. The smell of gasoline is strong as I make my way past the pumps. There's a convenience store with an entrance on the outside and then inside contains a food court and restrooms. The brisk night air is the only comfort against my hot skin.

Evan, a man taller than me and with more years in the bureau too, climbs out behind me and yells for me to wait up. The walk with him is silent and I know he's catching on to the tension but he gives me my space. Lord knows Evan has his own secrets and if the man is good at anything, it's respecting boundaries.

This time of night, there are fewer families in the rest stops than during the day, but this particular one has never been empty any time we've stopped here.

The interior is littered with cheap tables that are half-filled and the smell of burgers and fried food lingers in the air. There's only one corner relatively vacant and I pick that one, ignoring Evan's questioning look as he heads for the restroom and I don't.

The legs of the chair grind against the speckled linoleum and I take a moment to compose myself before I call Delilah. The tips of my fingers are numb as fear and anger stir inside of me.

If he threatened her, I'll kill him. I'll find him and kill him. If anyone has a clue as to where Marcus hangs out, it's me.

I don't know where he lives or what he looks like, but with the information I've got, my team will find him. I'll come clean, for her. I'll confess everything.

If it wasn't him who left the note and he knows who's

after her... then we have an even bigger problem on our hands.

Her number's on speed dial and without thinking twice I hit number 8, my lucky number, swallowing thickly as I stare straight ahead, mindlessly watching two kids pull on their father's jacket, begging for a cookie that's larger than the size of their small hands. They're all the way across the food court, but everyone in here can hear their pleas.

The phone rings and rings and just when I think it's going to voicemail, Delilah answers.

"Cody," she says and the longing and relief contained in the single-word answer does something to me. My heart sinks but in a way that's difficult to describe.

"I'm sorry I wasn't there," I tell her first, dropping my gaze to the gray lacquered tabletop. *Fuck, I'm sorry for so much.* The truth goes unspoken.

"It's okay. I'm okay," she answers quickly. "They found the kid, he works for a pizzeria and he's the one who left the note. He said a woman asked him to drop it off for me. She told him she was my friend and it was an inside joke. He had no idea."

A kid and a woman? The man I knew years ago as Marcus would never have involved children in his work. Never. Maybe she was right in the last message she sent. Two different situations, both colliding. My instincts tell me Marcus, at the very least, knew she'd be threatened. He has a hand in every sin that occurs in our city and I don't believe he just happened to be there. If the last decade has taught me anything, it's that there's no such thing as coincidence.

"And Marcus?" Anger flares in my tone and I have to

close my eyes to keep it at bay. When I open them, Evan is across the court, watching me but remaining at a distance. I wave a hand in the air to let him know I'm all right, but he stays where he is, diligently keeping an eye on the surroundings.

I'll have to tell him something. I'll think of some excuse. A partial truth maybe. Something happened to a woman I'm seeing. She's shaken up and I need to get the hell home so I can help her. That'll do it. Only Evan, though. The entire team doesn't need to get wind of this.

When one of us is down, all of us pull together. But this? They can't go digging into this.

Delilah's inhale is easily heard on my end of the line before she says, "I only think the man who walked me to my car was Marcus because of the note he gave me. The number is untraceable, probably a burner and when they called no one answered. They tried to track it and they got nothing."

Of course he didn't answer. There's no way he wasn't watching her every move. He knows she told the cops what she suspects. I should feel terror at the realization because Marcus isn't known for having mercy, but he told me how he felt about her once.

He wouldn't touch her. He made that clear.

He better fucking not.

"You saw his face?" I question her, my hand forming a white-knuckled fist at my side. He's a sick fuck and a ruthless murderer. It doesn't make sense that I'm this calm. That I can hold back this much of what I'm feeling. Except for one little truth. One small detail I've never told anyone.

"Only his eyes. Caucasian male with blue eyes."

No one's ever seen his face but me; and back then, it was only a glimpse. The details of who Marcus is choke me as I force my body to relax in my seat. It's only to put Evan at ease. What is reflected on the outside is nothing at all like the turmoil that rages inside of me.

"Is someone with you?" I ask her, praying the security team had enough sense to take this seriously. If everything she's told me is true, all they have is a note from a man who said he was Marcus. On paper it's not a threat, but in reality, she should be terrified.

"They put four men on me and they have two teams on the case. One for the note and one for Marcus."

I can only nod, words refusing to slip through my tight throat. She says his name so easily. Marcus. If only she knew.

Biting back a bitter taste, I tell her I'm sorry again and that I'm coming home. "You'll stay with me."

"You don't have to do that. I'm having security—"

"You will go to my place and stay there until I'm home. Your apartment's not safe until you get a security system. I'll do the installation myself." There's no margin for negotiation in my tone and as I lean forward, my jaw clenched and lungs still, I know that's not the tone Delilah typically appreciates. Her silence at the demand confirms my suspicions.

"Do it for me," I plead with her, lowering my voice as I do. "You don't have a security system, you're in an apartment with neighbors everywhere. My place is on its own; there's no risk and I spent a fortune on the security system." The reasons line up in my head. It's a mistake for her to stay in that building. Marcus could be just one floor up and there isn't a damn thing we can do about it. "Please," I add for good measure.

"Text me your address." Her tone is reluctant.

"The security code is eight seven four three. Got it?" I ask her and rub the back of my neck.

"I got it. When will you be home?"

"We're driving back now. Just twelve hours to go. I promise I'll be there soon."

There's a shift between us. It's been happening for weeks now. It's easy to deny what's between us when we both go along with it. But there's no question that she means something to me and that I mean something to her.

What that is... we don't have the time to delve into it right now. I just want to feel her, to hold her and know she's safe.

"I'll protect you. I promise."

We end the call as if nothing's changed between us, but I know it has.

I'll see you soon doesn't capture the meaning of what I want to tell her.

With the call over, I watch Evan motion to someone outside. The guys are ready to go. Irritation consumes me. I need a fucking moment to figure out all this shit and get a grip. Years of history come back to me. The details of a man I said goodbye to and thought I'd never hear from again.

I motion to the bathroom to Evan and he tilts his chin in acknowledgment.

When I'm enclosed within a stall, I text a certain number knowing full well if this blows up, the evidence will be damning. It's the only number I have of his, though. And

I'm unwilling to not reach out and tell him I know what he did and that he crossed a line.

You went to her? He sees the message almost immediately but doesn't answer and it pisses me off. Someone enters the restroom as another person leaves. I need to wrap this up. *You weren't supposed to go near her.*

The responding text is immediate: *Neither were you.*

The sounds of a faucet being turned on, a distant cough and footsteps in the men's restroom turn to white noise as Marcus continues in a series of messages that drain the blood from my face, even as it heats to an unbearable degree.

Where are you now, when she needs you?

Don't answer that.

It doesn't matter.

I'll take it from here.

chapter fourteen

Delilah

STILL STARING OUTSIDE THE WINDOW, I END THE call with Cody. The phone is heavy in my hand and I find myself gripping it tighter than I should. With my left hand holding open the curtains, I let my eyes adjust to the dark night and take count of the men outside.

I invited them in, but that's against protocol. Fine. They can stay out there all night. I don't care what anyone else does at this point. I just want to be able to sleep.

Exhaustion and disbelief weigh me down as I pull my robe tighter around me. A hot shower didn't do a damn thing to calm my nerves. I'm so tired, I feel as if I could lie down and fall asleep in only seconds. But I know better. With the way my mind is reeling, I'll be lucky if I can keep my eyes closed when my head finally lands against the pillow.

Reluctantly, I grab an overnight bag and begin packing. I only take enough for one night. Cody said he'd be back tomorrow and that'll give him hours to install a security system up here. It's plenty of time and I'm not staying at his place for more than just tonight. Especially when it's only so that one of the two of us can have less to worry about.

We're… we're not boyfriend and girlfriend. We aren't anything but friends who wind up in bed together. I barely even know a personal thing about the man. Much less the state of his place. I don't even know if it's an apartment or a ranch house or… whatever it is. Hope is nonexistent but I'm praying for it. The truth? The real truth? Even with the men outside, I'm so fucking scared. I've never been this terrified in my entire life.

It comes with the territory. The nature of my business is to be met with threats and stare them down while demanding justice. But from what I know, Marcus has his own version of justice and I don't know where I fall in his eyes.

My breathing hitches remembering his steely gaze, but I keep moving, grabbing my earplugs, sleep bonnet, and lip moisturizer from the nightstand and tossing them into the small travel bag then zipping it up.

I pretend I'm not falling apart with every step. I keep moving, grabbing a sweater aimlessly and then two blouses for underneath. It's when I'm folding them, the note coming back into my mind and the knock at the door of my office playing back in my head, that I nearly lose all control. Marcus is one beast and the threat is another.

The half-full bag sags on my bed as I cover my face

with my hands and just breathe. I finally get dressed, and just breathe. *Just breathe.* It's only once I calm myself down that I realize my hands are shaking.

Hugging myself, I sit on the edge of the bed, rocking slowly and pulling myself together. I let myself slip off the side, falling to the floor and leaning my head back against the mattress.

I could call my sister, but it would frighten her more than anything. What good would that do? I could call my father and he would overreact. He would make demands and attempt to take over... not unlike the man I just ended my last call with, but at least I can go along with Cody's decisions.

I wish he were here. I need him and I don't want to need him like I do, but my God I do.

Is it so wrong to want to be held and protected? It goes against everything in my nature, everything I've worked for, but right now I desperately need it. A little human contact that reminds me I'm safe and okay and nothing bad is going to happen.

Because every time I close my eyes, all I see are the photographs from various crime scenes. But instead of the victim lying there, it's me. It's my eyes that are wide open, staring aimlessly and my body that's broken and lifeless.

Without thinking about it, I reach for my phone and text Cody as quickly as I can: *Please drive fast.* When it's sent, I can't take it back.

After wiping my eyes with a tissue and a handful of water splashed on my face, I give myself a cursory pass and pretend like none of that happened.

I take my time, reorganizing the bag and thinking about everything other than what happened tonight, grabbing some sleeping pills for safe measure before leaving my bedroom. I'm damn sure going to need them tonight.

Letting time pass, I go over everything I need and then do it again, making sure I didn't miss anything before zipping up the bag with a sound of finality echoing in the room. I saved a pair of gray sweats and a comfortable olive hoodie to wear tonight. I certainly don't look like a damsel in distress; I've never been a fan of that.

Taking deep breaths in and deep breaths out, I put on light makeup before making my way out of my bedroom, ready to relocate as per Cody's not so gentle request. The security detail will just have to follow me to Cody's place. I don't know what they'll think about it or if it goes against protocol, but I don't have the energy to fight and they can't make me stay here, so… it's up to them if they come or not. The last thing I'm going to do right now is fight with the only person I can confide in.

I don't want to be alone either, though.

With the straps digging into my shoulder, I carry the heavy bag past the kitchen and the bright bloom of gorgeous red petals catch my eye.

Roses. Dozens of roses.

The heavy duffle bag slips from its place and plops onto the wood floors. I'm still in bare feet and my soles pad on the floor as I make my way over. My first reaction is to touch the petals. They're velvety soft and the flowers are fragrant. There are at least two dozen roses in a simple vase.

Knock, knock, knock, there's a knock at my front door. The loud bangs startle me, forcing my fingers to pull back, not unlike Belle when the Beast came up from behind her, but I make haste getting to the front door, and see Taylor in the peephole. I could laugh at the reference to a fairytale; oh, what a poor excuse for a princess I would make.

I don't have to wonder why Taylor's here from the look in his eyes. Before I've finished opening the door, he's already started talking.

"I got a call from Agent Walsh about a relocation?" he questions. The quizzical look is paired with a knowing one. Swallowing a bit of embarrassment, I nod and then look him in the eye before I say, "He insisted."

There's a pause, and for a moment I imagine Taylor is going to question further, but he doesn't. "All right then. We're ready when you are."

"I just need five minutes," I tell him. Before he can fully turn his back to me to walk back down my front yard path the way he came, I ask, "Who brought the roses?"

"What?" he says and a cold chill flows over my neck and down further. Fear threatens to derail my composure. *How could he not know about the roses?* "What roses?" he asks when I don't say anything.

Opening the door wider, I ask him to come inside with me. "Is everything all right?" Taylor questions as he reaches for his gun.

I don't know. An awful sickness washes through me. It's not possible that someone came in here while the men were watching the place. It's not possible. My imagination goes a step further, questioning if the roses were here all along. They must have been. I was so out of it that I had to have missed them. Right?

Sensing how off I am, Taylor uses his transmitter to update the men that he's going inside and to do a sweep of the interior. I'm numb as I watch Taylor search through my apartment and then he checks each lock. Only the sounds of Taylor moving quietly and quickly from room to room accompany this horrible feeling that grips me like a vise. I only break away when he says there's no one else here. Searching the flowers for the card from earlier, I find nothing. *Where did it go?*

Holstering his gun, Taylor questions lowly, calmly but with authority, "Were they here when we got here earlier?"

"They couldn't have been," I answer in a whisper, but my head shakes subconsciously. Maybe it's disagreeing with me. "I don't know."

I've never felt so helpless and foolish all at once. "It's been a long day." Taylor's comment is meant to be consoling but it only adds to my humiliation.

With one last look at the roses, I let Taylor take my bag and follow him out to an unmarked black sedan, sliding in the back of it. My hands are still shaking, so I hold them tight and shove them between my knees the entire way to Cody's place. That's why I wasn't holding my phone; it's why I didn't see I had a new text until I was safely tucked away in Cody's home.

It's from a new number, one not in my contacts and I nearly drop the phone when I read the series of messages he sent me.

I didn't mean to startle you with the roses.
I meant it when I said I'd protect you.
No one will hurt you, my Delilah.

I had to change my number. Don't give this one away like you did the last.

chapter fifteen

Cody

I'M A HELPLESS PRICK. THAT'S ALL I COULD THINK the entire ride. Sitting in the back of a van, not able to do a damn thing but think.

I offered to drive, to do something rather than sit here being useless, but Bradley wouldn't let me. Evan hasn't pried, but I notice how he keeps glancing at me. If I noticed, so did everyone else.

Maybe that's why it's so fucking quiet.

Pretending that I'm on my phone only works for so long before the guys pick up on the air around me. Then I pull out some paperwork. Even as the vehicle jostles over potholes, I stare down at the black words on stark white pages and give my best effort to appear that I give a shit about what's in the files. It doesn't throw them off, but the message comes across loud and clear: don't fucking ask.

I can't think of anything else but her. Delilah.

Her and the man I've strategically aligned myself with. It happened so slowly, so carefully that I didn't realize what I'd done and how deep down the hole I'd gone until it was too late. There's no going back from the things that I've done.

I remember the first time I met the man who calls himself Marcus. Met… isn't the right word. It was the first time I came into contact with him. That's a better way of putting it.

Memories of the stench of that back alley behind an old strip joint on the east side come back to me as the van moves over yet another pothole and I'm tempted to cover my nose with the inside of my elbow like I did back then. It hit me hard, the smell of rotten garbage overflowing in the alley where the body was found. The steel cans were missing their lids and the ruined cobblestone streets the city refused to pay to fix were the highlights of that part of the city five years ago. I heard they cleaned it up some now, but back then, it was a hellish place to live.

If you found yourself that far toward the bay, it was best to go any other direction but east as quickly as you could. It was my third year on this job and my patience had worn thin on a series of murders we all knew were hits from a local mafia organization.

Everyone knew, but no one talked. Cuffed and placed in holding, all anyone said was that they wanted their law-yer if they were being charged. And if they weren't being charged, they didn't have a damn thing to say and wanted to be released. Being in holding for forty-eight hours didn't break down a single man. In a city like that, where everyone's down on their luck and the one place to find a hot meal is funded by a man who runs the streets... well, it was impossible to get anyone to turn on them. They all asked for the same lawyer, the mob's lawyer.

So when this body showed up, and no one saw anything and no one had anything to say but *get off my porch*, it wasn't surprising.

The body had been there for at least three days and when the trash bag that covered it was removed, the stench only got worse. I remember how my partner at the time had heaved, nearly puking right there on the body. That would have been damn awful for evidence.

My partner was much older than me and constantly bitched about wanting to retire and stop living a waking nightmare day in and day out. He was offered retirement last year, but from what I heard, he turned it down. I remember thinking back then, there's no way out of this. The work will stay with you long after the badge hits the bottom of a drawer.

I sent the old man away when we got to the scene and he gagged; we didn't need two of us back in the alley while we waited for backup and transport for the body. Sirens were a constant, and one bellowed behind us as he headed toward the street. The sun was setting. I watched it fall for a moment and did my best to avoid making eye contact with an older woman who peeked out of her curtains three stories up in the worn brick apartments across the street. She wouldn't talk, I knew that much. I also knew everyone fed information to the mob. If a person breathed in that town, they did the dirty work of Romano. Whether out of fear or a need to survive, I didn't know and I still don't.

I had an evidence bag in my hand, ready to pick up a necklace that looked like it'd been ripped from the woman. A thin red gash colored her neck and the silver chain was dull with dried blood as the streetlights flickered on.

"Shame, isn't it?" I heard Marcus before I saw him. He's good at sneaking around and hiding in shadows. Monsters like him all do the same.

With a hand on my holster, I heard the familiar sound of a bullet being chambered in a Glock. He tsked me as I stood there, painfully still, with my blood rushing in my ears.

"Don't do anything stupid."

I could try to pull out my weapon, and probably get shot. I could call out for my partner and probably get us both killed. Instead, I stared down at the woman's face and held my breath waiting for his next move. I didn't know where he was. Somewhere above me and to the left judging by how his voice carried. The alley sat between buildings with shops on street level and apartments five stories up. Back then I assumed he was watching from a window in one of those apartments. He had the upper hand and the cold sweat on the back of my neck made me all too aware that I knew he was the one in control.

He told me not to turn around, right before I heard the thud of a man jump and land behind me. The sun may have been setting but there was enough daylight to see him if I dared to disobey.

"Who are you?" I questioned, although I had an in-kling. We'd been keeping tabs on the local mafia for a while; we knew the real names of their members, had files on their whereabouts and aliases. There was one name that was only whispered. A rumor, a ghost. A single name and no other information save a list of bodies the people around here credited to him. We thought he was an assassin but as the truth unfolded over the years, I learned he was more than that. He was an angel of death. A murderer who killed based on his own morals and judgment. The chills flowing down my arms and the way he spoke made the name resonate in my mind before he spoke. When I first started, I thought the man didn't exist, but years in that town made one thing very clear. Monsters are real and the one named Marcus was the worst of them.

Marcus, he answered me and I knew the man behind me was a wanted serial killer who caused fear to run down the spines of even the hardest men from the mob that we'd interviewed. They called him the grim reaper, the monster under your bed. They called him a lot of things, but they only ever whispered his name in a single hiss.

He didn't stop to ask my name; he didn't ask me anything at all, merely made a comment about the dead woman followed by a sucking sound of discontent. And how it wasn't supposed to be her.

"What do you mean it wasn't supposed to be her?" I downplayed my interest as best I could, all while trying to conceal the nerves that rattled me and the fear that forced me to stare down the alley the way my partner had gone. I was alone with a man I couldn't see who held a gun at my back.

It was quiet for a long moment. Too many seconds passed for my liking. "I don't know that I can trust you yet."

"Are you going to kill me?" I didn't give myself conscious permission to ask, yet I did. I didn't want to die. Sure as hell not in some dirty alley with a gunshot to the back of the head.

"Why would I kill you? You want what I want."

I didn't answer and I didn't need to. All Marcus did was direct my next steps.

"Go down this alley and make a left at the corner store. You'll see it if you're looking for it."

"Looking for what?"

"For the weapon that ties Romano's predecessor to the crime scene."

Adrenaline spiked in my blood and I nearly turned to face him but the tsk and reminder of the gun he held kept me firmly placed where I was. I didn't trust him and I can't say that's changed much, even with everything I've learned.

I asked the obvious question, my eyes narrowing although they still looked at nothing in particular. "Why are you helping me?"

"I told you." As I stared at the crumbling brick wall in front of me, I heard him start to walk away as he spoke to my back. "We both want the same thing. It's hard to admit, but in this instance... I need you. And you don't have to admit it, but I know damn well that you need me."

Those were his parting words to me.

My partner strolled back not a minute after, two detectives in tow.

"You look like shit," he commented and the other two laughed.

Coldness surrounded every inch of me. It happened so quickly, I nearly thought I'd lost it. I could have told them what happened, but I didn't. Instead, when one suggested it was the odor that made me look so pale, I told them I needed a walk. I followed Marcus's advice and we nailed the son of a bitch who killed that woman and tied four other murders to him. We couldn't get Romano but Marcus told me later he had a plan and Romano was useful for it. Instead, he offered me a list. Letters came and kept coming. And I kept responding as the bodies piled up at my feet.

chapter

sixteen

Delilah

CODY'S COFFEE MAKER SPEWS AS IT SPITS OUT the last bit of coffee to fill the plain white cup. It's this high-pitched sound and I'm all too aware of it as I stare at the sputtering machine flicking droplets of brown liquid against the upper sides of the bistro mug.

It's damn good coffee though, strong but not bitter, and even the smell of it helps me to wake up just a bit more.

As I set the mug against the gray, speckled counter and reach for the sugar, I try to remember if this is my third or fourth cup. My conclusion as I pour far too much sugar into the mug, is that I haven't got a clue.

After stirring in a bit of creamer, the spoon clinks against the mug and I leave it on the napkin I put down this morning that's already stained with a round ring of chestnut coloring.

With my back to the counter, I blow across the hot cup and take in the expansive kitchen. It's just like the rest of Cody's single-floor ranch home: modern, monochromatic with all blacks, grays and whites, and hardly any personalization whatsoever.

Everything is updated and top of the line. The simple lights that hang down are sleek and look expensive. But there's not a single item on the counter, except for a toaster that looks brand new, the coffee maker, and now a stained napkin and spoon. This place is barren. It's too empty to even serve as a model home.

I breathe in the delicious fragrance and then take a short sip. It's comforting and tastes like home so I indulge in a longer sip next.

All night, I thought about every case I ever worked on where Marcus's name was mentioned. It's more than a few dozen of them. At least one hundred. A hundred times his name was implicated in some way or another. I used to think of him as the boogeyman. Some made-up horror story that criminals blamed when really, he didn't exist.

A number of times last night, my mind drifted to the roses he gifted me, which are now where I left them at home. But the red quickly bled into crime scene photos. Pools of blood and then their eyes, followed by his sharp blue gaze. I didn't tell anyone. I can't write it down or speak the reality. He was there in my most private of spaces. And what's worse is that he saw my reaction. I'll tell Cody when he's here, but for now, the confession is stuck with disbelief at the back of my throat.

There's one other reason... one I'm ashamed to admit, as to why I didn't tell a soul he'd messaged. *I have a lead.* I couldn't breathe, I couldn't speak; all I knew was I had a lead and sharing it with anyone else would ruin it. How fucking reckless is that? It's buried at the back of my mind, but the reasoning is very much there. Marcus is a wanted man... and I have a lead.

A lead and a vase of flowers.

The sight of roses turning into blood is the image that snapped my eyes open each time I tried to rest. It was like Marcus was watching me. I've convinced myself the pale blue of his eyes must be due to contacts. They're simply far too blue, far too beautiful.

Ping.

My phone dings on the counter. Setting my mug down I click on the screen to see it's another message from my sister. As if fate couldn't be any bigger of a bitch.

I've gotten three messages already today.

My mother left my father. She's an emotional wreck and my sister is in shambles even though for years she's been saying they aren't good for each other. Of course they need me now. Of all times, my sister wants me to come home *right now*.

She's practically demanding it and holding the fact that all I do is work over my head.

Hell... if she only knew.

The first time my phone went off this morning, I was making my first cup of coffee and I stared at my phone on the other end of the island where I'd decided to work. It couldn't have been any later than 6:00 a.m. My initial thought when the chime went off was: it's Marcus.

There was a hiss in the back of my mind, one provoked by the memory of his fingers against mine in the parking garage. One that taunted me. One that claimed I didn't tell anyone because it was my secret to keep. No one else was allowed to have it.

I'm only faintly aware of that voice. It can so easily be blamed on the lack of sleep and the loneliness that crept up on me in Cody's large, cold bed covered with black cotton sheets and a white and slate striped comforter.

The only bit of personality in that room was due to the full shelf of books. They're classics and their spines worn down. The one that made me smile was *The Hound of the Baskervilles*. It figures that Cody would like Sherlock Holmes.

I tossed and turned in that empty bed, doing everything I could to rid the day from the deepest, darkest places of my conscience. I even took four of those sleeping pills I packed, but they didn't do a damn thing.

I crawled out of bed and was met with that text from my sister, then one from Claire telling me to work from home today.

They don't want me back in the office until they have more information on who is really responsible for the note left at my door, a.k.a. a lead.

It was easy enough to agree and keep my feet planted in Cody's place. Not that I can focus enough to actually work. All I can think about is the phone number, each digit burning into my memory.

I haven't messaged Marcus; I haven't told anyone about it. Those four sentences feel like a ticking time bomb, and I don't know how to find the wires, let alone cut them to prevent inevitable ruin.

My sister's constant texts are the cherry on top of this shit sundae. At that very thought, another comes in:

I mean it, Dee. She won't stop crying. She's hysterical.

My sinking heart drags every cord down as it drops, stretching out the agony of it all.

Sometimes we see things we shouldn't. We go through moments that take ahold of us. That's the only way I can explain how I've felt since last night. It's not detached, it's overwhelmed. There was a time, when I first started, that I had to watch video evidence of a woman being beaten to death. It was only minutes and in this field, it wasn't the most gruesome thing I'd ever seen. But there was a child present, and he couldn't have been more than three years old. He was screaming and crying. He hit the man who was beating the woman. He wasn't even her son.

I wasn't right for a while. Days, maybe a week or two. I heard what people said to me but it took a moment too long to process, because all I could hear were the cries of a child wanting the bad man to go away. I understood how I felt, but the way my body responded and the way my thoughts weren't keeping up, I just wasn't right. My mind was stuck on the sound of a small boy crying out in time with the crunch of the woman's skull hitting the concrete pavement.

I can take a lot. I like to believe I'm a strong woman, but I'm slipping just like I did then, only now it's so much worse and seemingly slower. I'm slowly falling into a place I don't want to be and I don't know how to stop it. There's no side of a well to cling to… I'm simply falling into an abyss.

My phone pings again; it's my sister guilting me into taking time off since I hardly ever come home anymore.

I wish that I could. I wish I could just pause all of this shit like I did that video in the back office when I first started crying. Freeze it in time and let it turn stale while I go back home as if nothing's wrong. As if there isn't a security detail on my ass and a serial killer telling me he'll protect me. Calling me his. *His Delilah.*

A shiver snakes its way down my back, leaving a chill in its wake that even the hot coffee can't undo. Maybe I could leave and all of this would simply pause. Maybe Cody could come with me up to my sister's. He should be back now any minute. He could stay by my side and protect me from all the warring thoughts in my head. Maybe he'd even call me his. *Now I know I'm dreaming.*

With a roll of my tired eyes, I shake it all off. The self-pity and delusions combined.

I type back a message and then delete it: *I wish I could.*

I will talk to my boss and find a way. That's the response I settle on. Cadence thanks me, says she loves me. All the while I know I'm a liar. I could confess it all and tell her there's no way I'd risk bringing the mess I'm in to her doorstep, adding to her madness, or I can stay the workaholic sister who's trying but failing, and never comes home. I choose the latter.

The thud of my phone hitting the counter comes just before a creak of a wooden floorboard. It's a sound that freezes everything inside of me. With my body still, my eyes locked on the doorway it came from, I can barely breathe.

Someone's in the house. I can just barely make out their shadow.

The shadow shifts along the stark white wall in the

hallway and before I can move, I hear his voice. The voice that haunted me last night says, "I already took your gun."

My back heel had pivoted, the desperate need for a defense already decided, but with a harsh swallow, I stand firm where I am, attempting to calm myself.

"You said you wouldn't hurt me," I manage to speak, my voice tighter than I'd like, but it comes out loud enough.

My gaze flickers to the butcher block. I could at the very least, arm myself with a steak knife. He called me his, he left me flowers, but this man is deranged.

"Never." His answer is spoken with conviction and I'm once again pulled to the shadow that's stopped in the hallway just beyond the kitchen. The bright daylight has dimmed, but there's plenty shining through the window, enough to see the outline of a tall man with broad shoulders.

I remember the security guard, his sheer size and the balls he had to have to walk beside me.

Swallowing thickly, I question him, "Then why take my gun?" I even shrug, as if I wouldn't use it. As if I believe him for one second when he says he won't hurt me.

His chuckle is unexpected because it comes out so easily. A second passes and my heart hammers wildly, not at all enjoying his amusement. "You know why, Delilah. Let's not play games; our time is limited."

"What do you want?"

Tick, tock, thump, thump; my heartbeat races as I wait for the man to do something or say something. Time goes by far too slowly.

Roses. Red. Blood. Roses. Red. Blood.

Again I'm bombarded by images and confronted with

the gruesome reality, unable to pretend I'm not terrified. "Please don't hurt me," I say, and my plea is joined by a half-backward step of my bare feet on the floor.

I've never wanted to run so much in my life.

"Nothing I want to do to you involves pain." Marcus's answer calms the fight-or-flight instinct just barely.

"What do you want?" I repeat the question, attempting to numb myself as I trace the outline of his shadow with my eyes and inwardly curse Cody. *How could he have gotten in here? How utterly useless is this protective detail?*

"The note, it came from the desk of a man called Herman." Marcus seems to huff a laugh at the name.

"Herman threatened me?" I ask quietly and calmly, although every inch of my skin pricks with fear. With my head tilted, and my voice sounding subservient more than anything, I brace myself with a hand on the counter and it takes every fiber of my being to listen. I settle on telling him the truth.

"Herman. I don't know a Herman."

I sound ridiculous to my own ears. I like to think of myself as a good actress under pressure, but my abilities seem to be failing me.

"He was hired to protect them. He paid off the cops who tampered with the evidence of your case that was just dismissed."

"The case against Ross Brass?" I question, little pieces of the puzzle falling into place. My tired mind catching up on details. Ross Brass was let go after evidence was handled improperly. "Ross paid this man to get him off and to threaten me?"

"Yes."

"Why threaten me? Why—" Before I can practically fall into the familiar steps of conducting an interrogation to uncover motive, Marcus answers simply. As he speaks, his shadow shifts, and the floor creaking drags my gaze back to him.

"Because you mocked him. You bruised his sensitive ego. Apparently he doesn't like the notion of rotting in hell." His words sink in, my mind finally filled in and crisper than it was ten minutes ago. I'm not certain I believe Marcus. To threaten someone under the DEA... after he got off scot-free? He'd have to be an idiot to do it.

"How do you know that?"

"Because I do."

"How can I prove that?"

His answer comes just as quickly as my question. A tit for tat, a back-and-forth. Although I don't care for his conclusion. "You can't."

The revelation sits between us, the air thickening. My initial thought was that the threat was from Ross in some way, but not directly. A fan or an accomplice. *If they rot, you rot with them.*

"You didn't sleep and I thought the information would give you some peace." Marcus's comment brings me back to the present. To the other monster taking control of my life.

"That's why you're here?"

"That and to tell you those men outside are unreliable and can't be trusted."

"If they knew you were here—"

"They wouldn't do anything because Taylor's right-hand man works for Brass. He's in his pocket."

"No—"

He cuts me off, saying, "Taylor you can trust, but I wouldn't count on the others."

He's met with silence as the heat kicks on and I'm suddenly very aware of how the lowered temperature has wrapped itself around me.

"I'll protect you."

"Why?" The single word leaves me breathless as I stare at the unmoving shadow. *Why me? Why does he care?* I have to ask and fear settles inside of me, knowing that wasn't the right move. For some mysterious reason, this man feels a connection between us; I'm only safe because of that. With a cold sweat lingering on my skin, I know I've messed up.

Marcus doesn't answer. Instead he says something entirely unexpected.

"I know you're going to want to tell him. You trust Cody more than me. I'm all right with that. I accept it and he'll be able to pull strings I can't. Tell him."

There's a pain etched in his voice and I hate that I feel sympathy. I shouldn't feel anything for this man.

The shadow moves, an arm raising as he adds, "I'm going to leave a USB flash drive with some files for you."

"Why are you helping me?" I question him further, needing an answer. *Tell me the truth, Marcus,* a voice pleads in the back of my head.

He ignores me, taking a small step forward as he says, "I want you to close your eyes and when you do, I'm going to come near you."

My heart pounds and my throat tightens.

"You won't open your eyes."

It takes great effort not to step backward as Marcus

moves forward again, only a single step.

"Keep them closed," Marcus commands and I can only nod, fear stealing my voice.

He takes another step forward, blue jeans coming into view and my eyes close. With my hands fisted, I grip my cotton tank top to keep from moving.

"Stay still and keep them closed." This time when he speaks, his voice is clearer and his steps easy to place. There's a clink on the counter; I imagine he's set the flash drive down there but then he takes another step forward.

"I give you something, and I'd like something, Delilah." His soft voice is comforting, a soothing balm although it barely penetrates the nerves.

I can only nod.

Another step, and then another. I count them in my head until I can feel the heat of his body and the presence of his shadow over me, blocking the light, wrapping me in darkness.

"I'm going to cover your eyes with my hand," he tells me and then adds, "And then I'm going to kiss you."

My fists tighten and my lips part just slightly, maybe to object, I don't know but it all happens too fast.

My feet move backward, his steps just as fast as mine, until my back hits the fridge. His hand presses against my eyes and his other at my hip, pinning me there as his lips meet mine.

Soft, yet demanding. It's all too hot and overwhelming. His body pressed against me sends a bolt of longing through me as he molds his lips to mine and groans deep and low in his chest. The vibrations only add to the flick of desire that comes with the flames of danger.

With his hand still firmly over my eyes, my back against the unforgivingly hard appliance and Marcus's grip digging into my hip, I stand there breathless, nearly shaking.

His teeth rake down the side of my neck and a gasp escapes me. True want and need roll through my body.

Shocked and breathless, attempting to cope with my own reaction, I stand there helpless just as I am, listening to him leave with haste and without a single word. I can still feel every inch of him: his heat, his demanding touch, and the all-consuming kiss.

It was only a kiss. If I tell myself that enough, one day I may believe it.

chapter
seventeen

Delilah

I WASN'T IN MY RIGHT MIND. I HAVEN'T BEEN. THE haze of whatever came over me, the sleeplessness and the reckless, wild thoughts, all vanish once my skin chills and the reality slams into me like a car without brakes.

I wasn't in my right mind. I couldn't have been.

It's all I can think as my hands shake at my sides. I've been staring at the cup of coffee on the counter as if it's the coffee's fault. Maybe it was drugged or poisoned. Because there's no way in hell that I just kissed a serial killer and felt anything other than disgust.

My mind is playing tricks on me.

The thought has my trembling fingers barely brushing along my bottom lip, where the kiss still sears my skin.

The creak of the front door opening forces a silent gasp from me as my wide eyes stare at the kitchen threshold. My body's so stiff, I can't do a damn thing but stare with bated breath. I only exhale when I hear my name called out by a familiar voice.

"Delilah." Cody says my name and as it echoes, I grip my right hand with my left to keep it from shaking as much as it is. Eyes closed and head down, I tell myself over and over: It's just Cody. Cody's here.

Oh thank God.

"Here," I say. My own voice contains tremors and I clear my throat. "I'm in here," I try to speak loud enough for him to hear me, but my voice falls, and my gaze turns toward the back of the house, in the direction Marcus left. I heard the door close. He's gone. I know he's gone. But how the fuck did he get in?

With confusion swirling in my mind, the tension and the disbelief still at war inside of me, I don't know what to do or say. The front door closes with a resounding click and heavy footsteps come fast toward me, getting louder until I can see Cody's foreboding figure in my periphery, the shadow of a man who I've desperately missed. His scent wraps around me in a comforting way, but it can't penetrate the strong feeling that engulfs every thought and emotion that rampage inside of me, wanting to scream, to do something!

Marcus was here. He kissed me. A serial killer was just here and I let him walk away.

"Gun, gun," I sputter out the word and keep staring down the long hall. "Marcus was here," I say although I don't know how I get the words out. "He was just here."

With my trembling hand I reach out to Cody, but it's useless. It's his strong back that greets me, pinning me against the counter. The marble digs into my lower back as I try to breathe, to get a grip on the here and now.

The sight of Marcus shrouded in darkness in the corner, my name on his lips...

"He's gone." I push out the words. "I heard the door shut and he said he was leaving. He's gone but he was just here."

"Which way did he go?" Cody questions with his back still facing me.

"He's gone," is all I can say and again I reach out, my fingernails digging into Cody's strong frame and my cheek slowly resting against the black leather of his jacket. I take in his warmth, his broad shoulders, his height and I try to cling to all of it. I try to reach normalcy again. The mindset I had before Marcus broke in and shattered my sanity.

Cody tries to move, to do something, presumably sweep the place, but I don't care what. I need him here. I need him close to me. "Stay. Please, please." I have to swallow the harsh ball that lingers at the back of my tongue. "Please don't move." My plea is a whisper and I feel myself losing it. He can't move. I just... I just need a moment.

"What did he do to you?" The question holds an air of its own darkness, a threat of what Cody would do to him. Cody turns ever so slightly to face me but still his eyes keep hold of the back hallway.

"Nothing," I lie in a quickly hissed answer. Why did I lie? Why hide the truth? Shame runs down my spine with a chill that rolls down my body and I find myself pulling away. My arms cross over my chest as I slip backward.

"What did he say to you?"

"Nothing," I repeat, feeling the spiked ball grow in an attempt to suffocate me. "Wait, no, no, he left information. He left it." My own story confuses me and I can imagine what it does to Cody. He doesn't answer for a moment, a long moment and I finally come back down from wherever I was, grounding myself and getting ahold of what happened. My eyes open slowly and I rest my head on Cody's chest. My lashes brush against the jacket while I'm staring at nothing, but seeing everything.

"Did you see him?"

Shaking my head against Cody's chest doesn't give him a quick enough answer. He turns fully, granting me his full attention as his arms wrap around my waist.

He kisses my hair and his body heat lingers, warming me slowly. Yes, this is what I need.

"Did you see him?" he repeats his question and I finally pull back, crossing my arms in front of me, the ghost of this reality still very much present.

"No," I say and shake my head again. "But I know it was him. It sounded like him and he knew things."

"What kind of things?" Cody's tone shifts. It's no longer comforting and it seems his interrogation is starting.

With his gaze narrowed and on me, I remember what happened. "He said he knew who left the note. A hired man from Brass. And he left the proof. He also said one of Taylor's men is in Brass's pocket."

"Shit," Cody sneers the curse, apparently believing Marcus instantly. "Taylor's crew is gone," he says and nods at his own decision, shifting his weight as his hand rubs the back of his neck. It's his tell when he knows shit has gone south and we have to pivot tactics. He truly does believe Marcus. With his eyes pinned on me, he repeats, "Taylor's crew is gone and I'll hire a new one. I know the firm. Consider it done."

It's hard to swallow, seeing the devotion and commitment Cody so obviously has to keeping me safe. My heart refuses to stay where it's supposed to, beating wildly. I don't have long before the moment is over, Cody hell-bent on taking control and quite honestly, I easily give it to him. With a nod, Cody seems to right himself, the man I know from work shifting back to the man I know from the bar and my bed.

"He *left* information?"

The single question stirs between us and I nod in the direction I heard the clink. Sure enough, a small metal USB flash drive lays there on the counter. "He said it would all be on it."

"Are you okay? All he did was come in here and deliver information?"

"That's all he did," I say then swallow harshly at the lie, doubling down on it and then I look into Cody's eyes, the shades of blue staring back at me with regret, remorse, but something more than that, something deeper. "He didn't hurt me. But it scared the shit out of me, Cody. I didn't have my gun and I thought I was safe here."

I ask the obvious question when silence sets in. "How did he get in here?"

Cody's gaze moves to the back hall once again and his jaw sets firmly in place. "Do you know how he got in? Window or door?"

"I don't know." I repeat myself as he stares down at me,

"I don't know." In the back of my mind I think it shouldn't matter, the security locks were engaged. The alarm should have gone off either way. Unless he knew the code.

It doesn't seem possible, but somehow Cody's large frame gets closer to me as his hands grip my shoulders. "You need to give me something about how he got in," he tells me, his sharp blue eyes begging me even though his statement is barely spoken, it's a dark whisper.

With one hand shoving his right hand off of me, I step away from him, regaining myself.

"I was standing right there," I say and point over by the coffee maker. "And I heard him before anything. He knew my name. He broke into my house yesterday." The sudden exposure, voicing out loud the lack of boundaries that man has, leaves me feeling numb all over.

"I know," he says and Cody's voice is gentle, consoling even. "I know he did that. He left roses. But that was yesterday and that was your apartment, not here…" his voice trails off and then he adds that Taylor told him. Taylor didn't know what to think, but Taylor hasn't worked against someone like Marcus before.

"You're sure you never saw him? He came close to you into this kitchen and you never saw him?"

It takes me a moment to realize he's questioning if I really saw what I saw. Is that what he's doing?

Spitefulness lingers in my tone. "He was standing right there," I practically yell, pointing to the corner. I'm quick to point out the evidence. The physical proof he was here. "He left this," I say and snatch the flash drive off the counter then shove it into Cody's chest. "He has the name of the man who left the threat in my office. He said he wants to help me."

My throat is raw from the indignation of my statements. The evidence lining up. "He was here, Cody! He came into your house and he could have hurt me, but he didn't." I keep from screaming only by forcing the words through clenched teeth. The tremors return, the anxiousness from knowing everything that could have happened.

When I look back up at Cody, resting my elbows on the counter in an attempt to steady myself, regret lays in his expression. It takes a moment before Cody's brow morphs into a straight line, leaving a deep crease in the center of his forehead. The anger that brews there for the man named Marcus only makes Agent Walsh look more protective.

"He came in here and left this for you? And that's all he did?" he questions again. And again I lie.

I nod yes, although it's a short-lived motion. "Yes, and then he left and you came. You came in right after. He just left. He was just here." My sentences tumble out at once and again I cross my arms in front of me protectively. Glancing from the corner where Marcus was and then back up to Cody.

"Are you okay?" he asks yet again and I watch the cords around his throat tighten as he swallows. I respond weakly, "Yes." I am okay. It's difficult for me to grasp. The grim reaper himself kissed me. The man who everyone fears *wanted* to kiss me.

"He didn't hurt you or threaten you?"

"No, he didn't. It was the opposite. He said he would help me. He promised to protect me. How did he get in here, Cody?" I ask the more pertinent question.

"I don't know." His answer is cold. "We need to get out of here and do a sweep."

"No, no, don't tell anyone." I'm quick to cut him off and then reach for his forearm when his shock and hesitancy are evident. "He has proof; he wants to work with... with us." I include Cody, praying he'll listen while a tingling sensation spreads through me that feels an awful lot like desperation. If Marcus knows who's after me... I would rather work with one devil, than die by the hand of another.

"Hire new guys and have them do a sweep for precaution. Hopefully figure out how the hell he got in. But don't tell them." I peer into his questioning gaze as I plead with him. "Please. I want to catch this guy as much as you, but if he knows who's after me..." I let my plea hang in the air, most of it unsaid as my heart bows in agony in my chest. *What am I doing? What am I even asking?*

"You need—"

With my hand on his, I leave only an inch between us, praying that he'll listen to me. "I know what I need. I know the look on your face. The look that you know better and that I'm not all right." I tilt my head up to meet his gaze and prove I'm all right, keeping my spine stiff and my shoulders squared.

"You want to make a deal with him? A deal with a murderer?" Cody doesn't hide the slight disgust, which adds another layer to my shame, but there's also a hint of hope. Because he didn't say no.

"There was no deal..." I whisper the lie, finding it hard to keep eye contact with the man in front of me. A man who came back here to help me. A man I lie in bed with. A man who right now, looks at me as if I've lost my mind.

After a moment of quiet, he questions, "Are you sure about this?"

I don't hesitate to answer yes. Swallowing thickly, I remember all of Brass's case. I remember it all and vengeance spurs inside of me. "If we could get Brass—"

Cody cuts me off, changing the dialogue between us as he says, "If we could get Marcus, it would be the end to three open cases and a string of murders."

"I know. I know."

"You're shaken up right now." Cody's strong hand lands on my shoulder, pulling me in closer and I pull away just slightly, hating that he's placating me.

"Come here, Delilah. As me and you. For the love of God, let me hold you."

"I don't want to tell." I offer up my end of the bargain and that's exactly what this is.

"Let me hold you." Cody repeats his, his brow lifting and his arms opening.

With my feet planted I tell him, "We aren't telling anyone anything and we need to see what's on that flash drive."

After a short pause of consideration, Cody agrees and pulls me in, telling me he's sorry he wasn't here. Murmuring all the right things and it's in his arms that I feel right again. My mind right and sound. But he can't hold me forever.

chapter eighteen

Cody

"I SAW YOUR APB. FIGURED YOU'D WANT TO come see this." Officer Brady nods his head as I walk carefully across the street while avoiding piles of litter and head to the back of the convenience store.

"Just put it in last night," I call out over the loud drone of traffic behind us. The APB for Herman Jackson went out the second I got his name from the flash drive Marcus sent. The fucker was as good as dead. Apparently someone else thought the same.

The city is bright and lively against the stark yellow tape I know so well, draping the crime scene and bringing in onlookers.

Brady lifts the tape and the two of us duck under. With my watch telling me it's 9:00 a.m., I know it's been an hour since the body was found. It took that long for me to get through morning traffic so I could see it for myself.

Someone offed Herman Jackson before I could. The rage that boils inside of me, knowing I can't question him, isn't unexpected.

"You sure it's him?" I question, keeping my pace with his as we avoid the trash bags and stand over the body. With his dark beard, height, and evidence of a long-ago broken nose, I know this is him. Herman's dead on the street in front of me.

Fuck. I stare to my right, hands on my hips as Brady pulls out the victim's wallet from an evidence bag to check for ID. The crowd doesn't try to hide their curiosity, but from this angle, I know they can't see a damn thing.

After I hired Evan's crew, we did a full sweep, we checked the camera footage. Bastard must've had Delilah's phone tapped when I told her the code. He was there before she even got there, turning off the cameras. I won't make that mistake again.

She's not allowed to be by herself. Whether she likes it or not. Dread eats me alive at the thought of Delilah and him being left alone together. She knows damn well what he's capable of; we both do.

It's not going to happen. It can't happen.

"Yeah well, judging by the body, he was already dead, probably forty-eight hours at most." Brady's voice brings me back to now. Back to the fact that this fucker was dead before Marcus even told Delilah about him.

I give Brady a nod, short and to the point. "You have any idea who did it?" Brady questions. He's a street cop who I've seen a handful of times. Enough that I know his name. I know he has a wife and kids, two, I think. Running a hand over the back of his head he adds, "If you've got any leads, I'll take them. Unless the FBI is taking this case from me?"

Clicking the side button to my phone with irritation, I note Marcus hasn't written back.

My own message to him sits there. *You crossed a line going to her. If you touch her, I'll kill you. I won't think twice about it.*

"This one's yours. He was only wanted for questioning. I put it out for a friend," I answer Brady, feeling a tightness linger in my chest.

"All right," he concedes, and another cop calls him over, back to the street side, her hand covering a phone and telling him someone needs him.

"You good here?" he asks me and I nod, patting his back for good measure. "Thanks, Brady."

Again I drift back to the texts, hating that he's one step ahead of me. Pain lingers in the message. Acts done in fear are harmful and lack intelligence. He told me that once and it stuck with me, because it's so fucking true. I never should have sent it. I gave him the edge. I can't deny that his willingness to approach Delilah scares me. What Marcus is capable of, terrifies me. Even if I feel pity for him. Even if I brought all this on…

"Walsh, you hear me?" Officer Brady questions, staring up at me from where he's now crouched on the ground next to the body.

"No, what's that?"

"There's a note if you want to take a look at it. Just in case it has to do with your case."

A note? Goosebumps spread in an instant, taking me back to the first case that I ever worked on where Marcus was involved.

Already tucked away in a ziplock plastic bag, Brady passes me the note.

It's not in his handwriting, it's in the font of a phone message. Same size too.

That motherfucker. It takes everything in me not to react when I read it. To stay calm and pretend to rack my brain for what it could mean when I know damn well it's from Marcus.

I'll be her hero this time.
The hero gets the kiss.

The coroner and another cop come up alongside us, distracting Brady for a moment as he watches them. With fire in my blood, I hand the note back to him, clearing my throat to get his attention. "Sorry man, I have no idea, but I'd get that to processing."

I'll be damn sure to keep an eye on the forensics for this case, but I already know it's a dead end.

There won't be any evidence. Marcus doesn't leave anything behind. He's too careful. All this was intended as a show for me.

"If you could keep me updated with the case, I'd appreciate it," I say then tilt my head to stare down at the body and add, "I want to know all of his connections."

"What is it you think he did?" Brady questions, standing up and wrinkling his nose from the stench.

I keep my tone as casual as I can. "He threatened a

lawyer I know, trying to cover up a case she was working on."

"How do you know it was him?"

"A kid IDed him." That was the first call I got. This was the second.

And there's not a damn thing I can do now, but question Ross Brass without a warrant. I already know how that will end.

chapter
nineteen

Delilah

With the suspect Herman dead, Claire didn't fight me when I said I wanted to get back to work. She did say I had to see the department psychologist first though. Luckily, he cleared me.

He doesn't know about Marcus and Claire doesn't either. That is, nothing apart from the incident in the parking garage and the suspicion that it may have been Marcus. The leading theory now is that it was someone hired by Herman. At least that's one of several.

Cody's on board to keep quiet about what happened between Marcus and me, plus the flash drive. It's not like we could use it in court anyway. It's inadmissible evidence because of how it was acquired. The kid IDing Herman we can use, though. Now it's just a matter of tying Herman to Brass.

The terminology "rot" is all I've got to work with and that's not enough for a warrant. I don't need a warrant to know that Herman worked closely with a man named Harrold Reynolds. He owns a dry cleaning business on Thirty-fourth Street. He was never a suspect in any case, but he was brought in countless times for questioning. His lawyer is familiar to our firm. He represents the mob.

It doesn't make sense. Or least it wouldn't without the bank accounts and proof of laundering. His former secretary is one of the women I suspected was murdered by Ross Brass, although I never did know why.

And there's the connection, if only I can find new evidence that wasn't tampered with that would lead Ross back to the secretary's murder, which connects him to Reynolds who is already connected to Herman. It could be my way in. My mind spins, going through everything just as it has all morning and afternoon well into the evening. Glancing at the clock in the upper right corner, it's already 8:00 p.m. It's time to go.

But the case doesn't quit.

Ross Brass committed a series of murders and got off on evidence tampering. The man whose release got me so worked up that I fell into a PR nightmare. I know he killed those girls… the laundering part is new, though.

Maybe Ross was the first man for hire. He isn't the starting point, so we'll have to look back further. I'm not sure, but the evidence on the flash drive files isn't enough. There are deposits to a number of bank accounts, but none can firmly be traced. Not without a warrant and I don't have evidence I can submit to get that warrant.

The theory: The mob hired Ross to launder. Ross used

the money and Harrold Reynolds to commit other crimes, eventually leading to murders. When he got caught, he hired Harrold's buddy, Herman, to get him off. It worked, but I pissed off Ross with my comment and Herman was hired again. Maybe I would have been murder number five. Maybe I still will be.

It's only a theory with weak connections. Still, it's a theory. My tired eyes stare at the white computer screen. There are so many pieces, so many crimes and only so much information I have that can go toward motive.

I click my phone on, wondering if I asked Marcus, would he tell me? Does he already know? Staring at his phone number listed under just the letter *M*, it feels like I have a direct line to the devil. It's unused. Not a message has been sent back to him since the first text two nights ago... But I have it. I could use it. I could nail that son of a bitch if only I had more to go on. If I could get my hands on something definitive that no judge can dismiss.

A ping from my phone catches me off guard, my anger waning at the sound.

Are you doing all right?

The text from Cody stares back at me.

Am I all right? No.

Cody can tell I'm not and I hope he thinks I'm off because I came in close contact with Marcus. He's got a hired man outside my door and it's... at best, distracting. At worst it's causing rumors and could be a potential lawsuit. *"If the DEA allowed someone to come back to work while under protection..."* Claire's warning from earlier today echoes in my head. Telling her my boyfriend is just being protective earned a laugh and then a stern, *"That better be all this is."*

Better than this morning, I message him back.

I don't know what to think or really, what I was thinking when it all happened.

The shrink this morning told me to "jot it all down." As if it's that easy. As if there are no repercussions. If I do, it's evidence. If I don't, I'm opening myself up to committing obstruction of justice. So, I haven't written a damn thing.

I text Cody again, even as I stare at the bottle of expensive white wine that was waiting for me when I got in here. *I'm fine. Not getting much work done, but I'm fine.*

It's a lie. When did I become such a liar? Every other sentence out of my mouth today has been a lie.

When Cody asked me if I was all right being alone. When Claire questioned if I was stable enough to come in. Not to mention the lying I did in the shrink's office.

Just thinking about that session has me eyeing the bottle of *Valley Pines* Pinot, my favorite wine, wanting to uncork it and have a long, slow sip of the sweet addiction. Hide away in a bottle and pretend like this past week never happened.

How can a small series of events over such a short period of time drastically affect me like this? They make me question who I am.

For instance, the wine. I know who it came from… and yet it remains where it is and I have every intention of drinking it. Maybe I felt unsafe at first.

I did what any normal person would do, what the previous version of myself would do.

I asked who brought it to my office. The bottle of red came in a pretty bag with a bow—and a note. *I thought you might need this.*

First roses, and now wine. It's another gift from Marcus. I know his handwriting now.

He watches me; he must. How else would he know that I keep wine in the office and more importantly, that I was out, confiding in the psychologist just so I could get back in here. It was the perfect opportunity for a delivery man to bring in a package and no one would object or question in broad daylight. No one was here who would have thought it was suspect. It's clearly a gift from a friend who heard what happened. I'm certain that's what they all thought. Bought and paid for by John Smith according to Greg, the delivery man who signed in and left the wine with security.

Instead of telling anyone, I added it to my growing pile of secrets.

Marcus gets into places he shouldn't be able to. He hides his identity with disguises and multiple aliases. Marcus is truly like a ghost. Coming and going as he pleases with no obligation to the laws the rest of us abide by.

So when I heard Herman was dead, naturally my mind put two and two together and I stared at the bottle of wine, willing it to spill more secrets like Marcus had.

I should be grateful that the man who worked to help threaten me is dead. A piece of me is. A small, ragged piece that broke off right about where I'm standing now while my fingers grazed over the threat that was embedded in that note.

But another piece of me feels... sick. And responsible. I can't help but to feel complicit in his murder. Not just because I wanted him to pay for what he did to me, but because I know things that no one else does.

No one but Cody... and Marcus.

The soft knock on my door is welcome, stealing me away from these thoughts and the trails my mind is leading me down. At first I think it's the security detail, wanting to know if I have an ETA for when we'll be home. Evan's already asked twice. It's not, though. It's Claire.

"What's going on with you?" Claire asks as she shuts the door, her black silk blouse reflecting the yellow light as she does. "Still shaken about the threat?" she asks with the soft click of the door shutting. A friend is what I need now. Thank God for Claire checking in on me before I lose it all.

Shaking my head no, which oddly enough is true, I answer, "Just focusing on Brass."

"The four murders?" she questions, touching on the cases he walked on.

"And the note. The threat I got."

"You really think Herman and Brass are connected? That Brass was behind it all?"

Yes. I do. Only because of Marcus. If I tell her I do... well, a good lawyer wouldn't jump to conclusions. "It's a hunch. I just want it solved."

"Understandable. Threats shouldn't be taken lightly," Claire answers easily as she gracefully takes the seat across from me. She adds, "A man like him doesn't stay out of trouble… so we'll nail him one day. Speaking of, did you hear Herman was found dead this morning?"

"Yeah, Walsh told me."

I don't miss the way her head tilts slightly and her arms cross against her chest when I admit that Walsh told me. It strikes me as odd. Why wouldn't he tell me?

She questions, "You think Brass did it?"

No. I think Marcus did. I think he did it for me. It's only a hunch, but I feel it deep in the marrow of my bones. Every time his name comes up, Marcus, a deep need runs over me to close my eyes. To remember the way his scent and his heat wrapped around me. If I'm not thinking about the details of the case… I'm thinking about him or pleading with Cody to keep me occupied.

I'm desperate to know how Marcus became the man he is. Did he really do everything everyone claimed he did? The questions bombard me once again and with them screaming in my head, I look back up at Claire and try to remember her question.

I'm fairly certain Marcus killed Herman. That's not what I answer, of course, and another lie slips out. "I think so. I think Brass knew the kid would ID him and he wanted to make sure Herman couldn't rat."

Claire nods. Her eyes are discerning though when she says, "It's a decent theory."

I can hear the questions she'd typically rattle off. Questions to get me thinking. They all start with the other man from that night. The man with the blue eyes who called himself Marcus. Ross Brass doesn't have blue eyes or fit the physical description.

She doesn't ask a single question, though. Not one and

that knowledge makes my skin heat with the sense that she knows I'm hiding something.

Or maybe that's just guilt.

I pause, leaning back in my chair, wishing I could tie Brass to Herman's death. It would be so easy. It would be justified. "The only thing we have is the ID of a kid," I tell her, breathing in deep and racking my brain for some evidence from the secretary's murder that would tie Herman and Brass together more closely. That's all I need and we can bring Brass in.

"And the dead body," Claire comments.

"Right, and a dead body."

"What about the note at the scene? Did Walsh tell you about that?" Her questions come back-to-back, berating me. I understand she's a bit overbearing given everything that happened. But she can back off of whatever trail she's on. She's dead wrong.

"No. He didn't. What note?" She doesn't answer me; instead she searches my eyes for something and whatever it is she's looking for, I don't think she finds it.

"To be frank, the only thing keeping you from being a suspect in his murder is your alibi with Taylor."

What? My eyes widen with both contempt and disbelief. "I know you wouldn't do something like that. But the fact that it came up at all as a theory... That's a little too close for my liking. Especially given it was only a month ago that the article came out and the animosity there. We don't need any more heat. You," she says while she points directly at me and I want to snap her finger off, "you don't need any more heat."

"I don't have anything to say to that." It's all I can

respond, ignoring her and the pissed-off feelings seeping through me.

"You're too close to this case." Claire's voice is gentle and I understand why, but it doesn't matter. She can't take me off this one. I know it better than anyone else here.

A huff of a laugh leaves me as I close my laptop, rubbing my eyes and knowing that's far too true. This case is everything.

"You need to take time off, see your sister or your mother." Claire's advice strikes a nerve with me for a number of reasons, but more than that, more guilt. Guilt on top of guilt.

Shit. Shit shit shit. That's exactly what I feel like right now. I never texted her back. In all the hours I stayed awake last night, refusing to close my eyes because every time I did, I could feel Marcus's hand pressed against them, I didn't once think about my sister.

I bet she hates me right now. I haven't even spoken to my mom. My heart swells with a pain I know too well.

"You can't focus." Claire interrupts my train of thought. "You aren't going to be productive here." Numbness crawls across my skin. I have to be here. I have access to everything here.

"All I have is my work." I tell her a single truth that she knows just as much as I do.

"Well, right now, you don't have that."

"What?" My blink is slow as my brow creases.

"I told you to go in for evaluation," she says and Claire's tone is accusatory.

"And I did," I answer pointedly. Where the hell is she going with this?

"And he said you aren't ready." Claire's arms cross, wrinkling her black blouse as it shifts from where it's tucked into her gray pencil skirt. "In his particular phrasing, 'her grip on reality is loose.'"

What does that mean? What the hell? That's not at all what he told me. "He signed off on me returning to work," I say and disbelief coats my response.

"Are you depressed? Anx—" Anger waging against any sense of reason, this time I cut her off.

"Depressed? Do I look depressed to you?" I question, truly taken aback. There's not an ounce of me that's depressed. I know I'm not with it, but depressed? Fuck that.

"Well, what is it then? You aren't yourself." The statement Claire gives comes complete with a flash of a man, only his shadow. My heartbeat slows and chills flow down my shoulders, but every other piece of me is hot as I attempt to breathe.

"I'm shaken up is all," I confess to Claire, to give her something that would change her mind. "Don't take this from me, please."

"How many times have you asked me that in the past few months?" Claire responds and it stings. "This Brass case has worked its way into your head, and I can't have it here. You need to go home."

"I was cleared—"

"You didn't tell him everything," Claire cuts me off, stern and to the point. Silence fills the space and my gaze drops to the bottle of wine. "So you aren't cleared."

My voice would shake if I were to speak right now, so I don't.

"It's just temporary. Go home, see your family." Claire's gaze burns into me but I don't return it. Not even when her tone morphs to something more consoling as she adds, "Just take care of yourself."

Cody wants me at his place, which is cold and the only heat I feel there when Cody's absent is from the memory of a man I should be terrified of.

How am I supposed to get better? How do I get through this if I'm not allowed to work on the case that's fucked me over?

The one-word answer is all I give her in response. "Fine." My tone denotes everything I'm feeling. Finality, betrayal. That fucking shrink cleared me.

I don't hesitate to put on my coat. There's no use in fighting and I'm not at all in the right mindset to argue. The last thing I want is to lose my job. That's something I would never recover from. With a tight throat and tension throughout my entire body, I ask, "How long?" My fingers are numb as I button my jacket. I can barely focus enough to do it although my back is turned to Claire, so the silver lining is that she can't see how unnerved I am. Even as I grab the bottle of wine, intent on drinking every last drop of it tonight, I hide everything I'm feeling.

"Come in next week for another psych evaluation."

Evaluation, my ass. If they really knew what was going on in my head...

I can only nod and as I go to leave, Claire calls out my name. "Delilah." My feet stay planted as I stop where I am but I don't turn back around when she tells me, "I'm doing this for your own good. You'll see that."

The words I want to reply tumble over each other at the back of my throat. Suffocating me as I leave the building, Evan following in tow, asking questions that I don't answer.

chapter twenty

Delilah

TO LOVE IS NEVER WRONG.

That's a phrase my mother told my grandmother years ago after an angry conversation that was taken to the kitchen.

I was only a little girl, but I remember it well. It's one of my first memories in fact.

Her voice shook when I peeked in the doorway to find her face-to-face with my grandmother whom I loved so much. I could tell she'd been crying and she told my grandmother, "To love is never wrong."

After recent events, I have some thoughts on that memory. But still, the words ring clear in my head. To love is never wrong.

Yet here I am, with feelings stirring for one man, one I

should certainly not be attracted to, let alone love... while sitting in the living room of another man.

It's not love. Not for either of them. I know it's not, but the longer I stay here, the more I can feel myself slipping.

Every sip of wine, in this empty place, only leads me to think of Marcus. And oh my Lord, my mother would eat her words if she knew what I was thinking. It would be sickening if I really did feel anything toward him. But I can't stop thinking about that searing kiss. I can't stop questioning, why me? And remembering all the notes from years ago. The closed cases that all led to one elusive man.

I don't know if it's shock or if it's PTSD but I've been in a daze since Marcus showed up and approached me.

Maybe even before then. When his fingers brushed against mine in the parking garage, when he left me flowers and then the kiss.

With a whirl of my wrist, the pale yellow wine swirls in the glass. It's my third and the bottle will be empty by the fourth.

I'd be ashamed if I gave a fuck. I can't go to work, so I've chosen not to go home and to stay at Cody's place instead. I'm out of my element, losing all control and therefore my mind.

There's a constant security detail present and every time I go outside they stand at attention, not speaking, just waiting. I feel like a prisoner more than anything.

Evan is nice enough, but he's gone, and I can't even remember the names of the two men out front. I decided tomorrow would be a better time to get acquainted more thoroughly. Tonight, the only interest I have is finding sleep at the bottom of this bottle.

So, sitting on my ass in the middle of the rug in Cody's living room and staring at the large modern art piece on the stark white wall is what I settled on when 10:00 p.m. rolled around and Cody said he had a lead and would be out later than he said he would. The black splotches that fade to gray don't say a damn thing. It's pretty. That's all it is. Monochrome and pretty to look at.

I down another sip, letting the sweet liquid pool on my tongue before slowly sucking it down. Another large gulp empties the glass and I stand up, stretching out my back and listening to the background noise of some cooking competition show that's on the large flat-screen TV behind me.

My head feels lighter, the tension in my shoulders nearly gone.

Nothing matters as I stare at the corner of the room where I first saw Marcus. Willing him back so I can question him the way they all question me.

So I can ask him why... why kiss me? Why help me?

More than that, what does he know about Cody Walsh? There's something there. I know there is. I can feel it. Like a gut instinct.

Of course, he would deny it. But didn't I deny it too? The dim light from the fridge gives a bit of warmth to the spartan kitchen as I grab the now nearly empty bottle and set it down on the marble counter with a loud clink. A softer clink follows with my wineglass.

I pour the last bit of wine and stare back up at the corner, trying to remember the silhouette of his body. With the memory, my eyes close and he touches me again. His hand wraps around my waist and—*Stop!*

Wrapping my fingers around the stem of the glass I hold it tightly as I sway where I stand.

I wish Cody were here. I wish I'd let him touch me and kiss me rather than pushing him away, which is exactly what I did last night. I need to wash the memories of Marcus off of me.

With a deep inhale, I take a look in the pantry, needing something of substance to help absorb the alcohol. Without something in my stomach, the thought of anything at all sounds scrumptious.

Three bags of tortilla chips and a loaf of bread are all that's there. Checking the fridge, I find similarly disappointing choices. And no salsa for the chips.

His pantry is evidence of one thing: Cody's never here, so it shouldn't surprise me.

Yet it does. I open a bag of chips and take it with me as I go, walking slowly and taking in every detail of Cody's place. It's sparsely furnished, one could argue it's a deliberately minimalistic style choice, but it's almost like the place is staged. Like no one really lives here.

There's a guest room with a bed and dresser. The bed is pristine, the sheets neatly tucked in as if housekeeping from a hotel had made it. I hesitate, eating a chip and staring at the black varnish before pulling out a drawer. Empty.

I toss the bag of chips on the bed and pull out another drawer and then another until I've looked through all of them. They're all empty.

The closet drawers are the next to be opened. Again, there's nothing but a folded spare blanket.

It is the guest room, after all. I doubt Cody has many guests. His uncle isn't well and doesn't like to travel. I can't even remember a single time Cody's spoken about someone coming to visit or stay with him. It's only ever him going back home.

The closet doors shut easily enough and I continue my exploration. When I put the half-empty bag of chips back in the pantry and glance at the red digital clock on the oven to find it's nearly 1:00 a.m., I'm empty-handed on any new information at all about Cody. There's nothing personal. Not even in his bedroom.

My tired eyes beg me to sleep. My mostly unsatisfied appetite begs me to eat. And my conscience begs for more wine.

Shutting the still-barren pantry door again, with the same amount of disappointment as before, leaves me staring down the hall at the half bath and the small closet just beside it. It's the last place to look and with nothing better to do and thoughts of Marcus still lingering and threatening to take over, I head to the narrow door.

The wooden shelves boast few toiletries and spare washcloths. His place is so bare, it's… uncanny. I've nearly closed the door when I realize there's a box on the very top shelf. It's unlike anything else in this place because it's a cardboard storage file box. Everything else seems luxurious, even if it's bare and minimal. But the box on the top shelf is dusty from years of sitting still. I can't reach it even though I try to and in my drunken state combined with boredom and… curiosity, I'm quick to grab the ottoman from the living room, drag it down the hall and get my hands on the box.

It's heavy, so heavy and the sharp edges force me to wince when they dig into my forearms. I nearly drop the thing and I'm glad I don't, because it's filled with papers but also a thin, hollow tin horse. It looks like it was once a piggy bank, but its detail makes it look like a trinket one would give to a newborn baby.

It's old and dingy, but I imagine once it was a beautiful gift at a baby shower. What the hell is it doing in a box that looks like crime scene evidence?

With the box on the ottoman, I sit beside it, cross-legged in my sweats and lift one of the straps to my tank top back into place. Confusion etches a deep line into the center of my forehead when I read adoption papers from almost forty years ago. Until I read the last name—Walsh.

First name: Christopher.

It must be a box of his brother's things. It looks like Cody's aunt legally adopted his brother after their parents died. Quickly I go through paper after paper, finding legal records, the criminal reports of his brother's abduction and an autopsy. My hands tremble and it's hard to read when my eyes water at the description of what was done to him. I can't imagine reading all of this and knowing your younger brother... Swallowing back the tears, I push through, needing to know more and understanding why Cody would hide this box away.

It's heartbreaking to the point that I almost miss the other names. The other boys who were abducted, including one named Marcus.

A sharp, frigid cold pricks down my spine and the lights seem darker as I read the black printed text on off-white paper, aged from sitting in a box, buried in a stack of articles that have yellowed.

Marcus Henry. The reports say he died but his body

was never found. Only teeth and bones, which the police took as evidence of his passing.

Only one child made it out alive. I knew that; Cody told me.

I can't shake the name of the smallest and youngest child, or his photo from evidence, barely a photo with how difficult it is to see his face, staring back at me in black and white. He's a little boy in an oversized baseball jersey, holding a bat. I can barely make out any details of him. But the writing is easily read. Only eight years old when the picture was taken, according to the script on the back of the photo. And next to his age, his name: Marcus. It can't be *him*. He's dead and it's just a name.

Rubbing both of my hands down my face I try to pull myself together. I wish I hadn't drunk the wine. I wish I could get the hell out of my own head. I can't breathe, I can barely see straight.

What the fuck am I doing? I shouldn't be going through Cody's things. This is a box of what he has left of his brother, I inwardly scold myself. Hating all of this.

He's protecting me and I'm violating his privacy. Oh my God, what came over me?

What the hell is wrong with me? As I frantically pile the papers in the stack they were in and place them back in the box, a small picture slips out, in black and white.

Two boys, with the tallest maybe ten years old, and the other a few years younger. Cody. Cody and his brother, Christopher, both the spitting image of the man behind them. Maybe their uncle.

The sight of the two of them together only heightens the guilt I have of betraying Cody's trust and rummaging through his things. What right do I have to go through his personal belongings?

Jesus Christ, what has gotten into me?

He lost his brother and these poor boys were murdered, yet here I am concocting some sort of connection with a man who broke in and kissed me in Cody's kitchen. I'm disgusted with myself. I've truly lost it. It's all I can think as I shake my head and brush away the tears from under my eyes.

I have to move the ottoman before I can shut the closet door. I'm halfway through the hallway, dragging the heavy thing back to the living room when I hear the front door open.

"Delilah?" Cody's voice is hesitant.

I don't call out, "In here," until the ottoman is back where it should be. My heart races and I know it looks like I've been crying when Cody steps into the doorframe, looking all sorts of the handsome man I fell for years ago. With grocery bags in both hands and shadows under his eyes, gratitude and unworthiness wrap themselves around me.

"Baby," he says and his voice drowns in agony as he drops the bags where he stands and eats up the distance between us before I can even take in a staggering breath. All I see in his face is his brother. "Why are you crying?"

I don't want to lie. I can't lie anymore, but I don't tell him the truth either, I simply shake my head, burying it into his chest and attempting to calm myself down.

This is what rock bottom must feel like.

I cry for him and for this craziness that's taken me over, but mostly I cry for his brother and the other little boys.

"I'm sorry," I finally answer and wipe away the tears.

I don't need to be even more of a mess than I already am. "I'm sorry, I just I couldn't sleep and I got to drinking." That's when I realize I didn't tell him about the wine. I didn't tell anyone.

With both palms pressed to my eyes, I pray for sanity. For all of this to end.

"Don't be sorry," Cody says then kisses my hair, and I rest my head against his shoulder as he rocks me, comforting me. And I know damn well I don't deserve it.

With that thought comes the nagging prick again. The one that tells me Cody knows more about Marcus than he's let on over the years. The pictures flash in my mind. And the realization dawns on me. *Why weren't there pictures of the other boys? Why was it all about Marcus and his brother?*

The nagging prick comes back as I stand there, feeling the chill of the air before the click of the heater comes on. I know Cody knows something. I know he does. I knew it the second I mentioned Marcus came to me. It's what's gotten into me.

Cody remains calm and comforting as the feeling of deceit takes over once again. This is what's making me crazy.

"I need to ask you something." My heart races as I give voice to words a part of me knows I shouldn't, not daring to look up. "I don't want you to lie to me, though." I pray I'm not wrong. If he doesn't know something for sure, he at least thinks it. He has a theory. I know he must. I can *feel* it.

"I won't," Cody swears, trying to look down at me but I cling to him, refusing to look up. "What do you know about Marcus that I don't?"

This story is only getting started. *This Love Hurts* continues with *But I Need You* and you won't want to miss this epic ride. Preorder your copy today of this breathtaking suspense!

Don't stop reading! If you haven't read the binge-worthy Merciless series, featuring an EPIC antihero brought to his knees, dive in today. It's the beginning of this world, a dark and modern retelling of a tale as old as time. You're going to love it!

about the author

Thank you so much for reading my romances. I'm just a stay at home mom and avid reader turned author and I couldn't be happier.

I hope you love my books as much as I do!

More by Willow Winters
www.willowwinterswrites.com/books